This novel is a work of fiction. Any references to real events, businesses, organizations, and political figures are intended to give the story a sense of reality and authenticity. Any resemblance to actual private persons, living or dead, is entirely coincidental.

Fool In The Ring

Copyright © 2019 – John Evans

All Rights Reserved.

Book design by Keith Katsikas

Cover design by Keith Katsikas

ISBN 978-1-9160418-2-0 (Paperback)

ISBN 978-1-9160418-3-7 (EBOOK)

1st Edition April 2019

www.johnevansauthor.com

DEDICATION-

Over the past ten years I have been blessed with a collection of very special friends, companions who have followed me on my journey through life. Two in particular have been a constant source of love and support. Leonardo and Alexis, the grace, love and fellowship you have given me is a gift beyond words or price. Your unwavering faith has brought me through some very dark times and without you, I would not be the man I am today and this novel would never have been written

Thank you

"Even in laughter the heart is sorrowful, and the end of that mirth is heaviness."

Proverbs 14:13
King James Bible

Prologue

The cars' headlights cut a swathe through the midnight darkness, panning left and right like relentless twin searchlights as the vehicle swept through the snaking twists and turns in the road.

Beachy Head Road was typical of most country roads in England, narrow, winding and treacherous for the unwary. It ran along the East Sussex coastline between Eastbourne and Birling Gap.

The vehicle, an old, dark blue, Volvo 200 series estate, thundered past the Beachy Head Hotel at a speed that belied its age, its big, diesel engine sounding like an old warhorse on full charge. The driver seemed oblivious to the apparent recklessness he was displaying as he threw the big, ponderous vehicle into a long, sweeping right hand bend that brought the road almost parallel with the coastline only a few hundred meters away.

As the Volvo came off the short straight and flew into the long left-hander its speedometer was touching ninety miles per hour and still climbing, yet the drivers' expression remained blank. He displayed none of the expected excitement nor exhilaration that would normally be associated with such actions.

The driver was unremarkable, if not for his fixed, trance-like expression he would have passed unnoticed. Close cropped, dark hair framed a vaguely oval face with no distinguishing features. His hands clamped to the steering wheel, knuckles white with the effort of maintaining control of the big machine. A plain gold band glinted on his left ring finger.

A short, straight section of road led into a tight right-hand bend. As the Volvo approached this it began to slow. Just past this bend the heavy estate suddenly swerved sharply off the road and onto a narrow parking area on the left side. It screeched to a halt, leaving a twin trail of rubber as it came to a juddering halt.

The drivers' side door opened and the man exited the vehicle. He was dressed in a plain, light grey, two piece suit with a white shirt and black shoes. While respectable, his clothing showed signs of wear. A slight fraying to the cuffs of his shirt and jacket, scuff marks on the front of his shoes, all served to indicate that his clothing was several years old and had seen a lot of use in that time.

The man left the vehicle with the door open, interior light on and the engine still running. He walked upright with sure, purposeful strides, heading across the parking area and onto the grassy fields leading towards the coast.

A steady breeze blew in from the sea, carrying with it the briny taste that was so familiar to coastal locations. This area was popular amongst hikers and holiday makers. During the day it was the perfect vantage point and It was along one of these time worn trails that the man now walked, heading directly towards the point where land and sea met.

There was no gentle transition between the two elements here. Over five hundred feet of chalky, white cliffs denoted the jaggy demarcation line. These chalk cliffs were the highest of their kind to be found anywhere along the English coastline. From land and sea alike, they were spectacular and were a major tourist attraction. Unfortunately, the sheer nature of the cliffs and the fact that they fell away, for the most part, directly into the sea, also meant that they offered an attraction of a more sinister nature.

It was only a few minutes' walk to the unstable edge of the cliff. There the man stood for several minutes, simply staring out to sea. He seemed oblivious to the wind which whipped around him with increased force, this close to the edge. Occasionally he was illuminated briefly in the baleful glow from the Beachy Head Lighthouse, just a short distance out to sea. The light atop its' conical tower like some ever watchful eye, constantly searching for unwary sailors, hoping to guide them away from the jagged coastline and back to the relative safety of deeper waters.

Eventually the mans' gaze was drawn inexorably downwards towards the crashing waves and barely concealed, jagged rocks below. The water foamed and sparkled in the pale moonlight, giving off a faint glow as the light was reflected back off the white chalk of the cliffs. The mans' hard, stone-like face gradually softened, his eyes revealing a deep, indescribable sorrow as a lone tear traced a sparkling path down his right cheek. He took a long, deep breath, then stepped forwards.

It took a little over five and a half seconds for the falling man to cover the distance. There was no sound, no screaming, and barely a disturbance in the turbulent water below to mark his passage. That short span of time was all it required to take a simple family man and convert him into just one more statistic, a footnote in the macabre history of Beachy Head.

The wind gained strength once more, carrying with it a new sound. It was just on the edge of hearing, a dark undertone to the gathering gusts that swirled around the top of the cliffs. Laughter, dark, maniacal, disturbing. It rose in pitch and volume briefly before becoming lost once more in the roar of the wind and waves.

13 | Fool In The Ring

Chapter 1

The late August sun fell slowly below the western skyline, bathing the ancient city of Bath in its warm, ruddy glow. Famous for its hot springs the town was originally called Aquae Sulis by the Romans and had stood since at least AD 60. Almost two thousand years later that same town had grown into a bustling city with a population in excess of one hundred and seventy-five thousand. The distinctive Georgian architecture crafted with local Bath Stone gave the town center a unique charm absent from other cities Hunt had visited recently. The effect of the deep red sunset on the usually honey colored stone was something that moved even his normally sour disposition.

Several months had passed since he had first woken from his coma back in his old, home town of Stoke-on-Trent. Even now Hunt found it difficult to accept just how much had changed in so short a time. The biggest change, he knew, lay within himself. He was now barely recognizable from the man he once was. His accident had left him horribly disfigured with the entire right side of his face looking as if someone had attacked it with a blow torch, melting skin and bone alike. Before he could fully come to terms with that however, it had changed again.

Hunt had acquired a power, an ability to control and manipulate the very essence of life. At the time he had been forced to use that power indiscriminately in order to save his own shattered body after being fatally shot in the head. He had killed people with this power, had drawn their very life force from their bodies and then had used that same force to repair his own damaged form. This energy had not only repaired the damage caused by the bullet that had killed him, it had also repaired the damage caused in his original accident. Bone, skin, muscle and nerve, it had all been regenerated to the point where all but the most observant of people would recognize that anything was amiss.

Hunt had not achieved complete normality in his appearance however. Along with his power over living energies, he had also developed an ability to see those energies as they flowed around all living things. It seemed that this ability had necessitated its own physical change. Hunts' right eye was now devoid of color, the white and pupil were normal but the dark brown iris had been drained completely, leaving it as clear as glass. This had proven too disturbing for people so Hunt had taken to wearing dark sunglasses permanently in an effort to mask this new feature.

Another item of clothing Hunt favored were gloves, thin, tight, black leather. He wore them constantly. Hunt believed that mastery of his new power required direct skin contact and, having lost control of himself once already, with devastating results, he was determined never to let that happen again.

Just over six weeks had passed since the events at the Exodus, during which time Hunt had tried vainly to come to terms with the new and frightening direction his life had taken. Upon leaving Andrew on that grassy, roadside verge outside the factory complex Hunts' initial response was to run away from it all, both mentally and physically.

He had returned home briefly, packed a small shoulder bag with a few essential clothes and other personal items, then left. Through a combination of walking and hitch-hiking Hunt had randomly crisscrossed the country over the last few weeks. He had no destination in mind, although his steps drew him inexorably southward, each step taking him further and further away from his old life. Drinking constantly now for need rather than pleasure, Hunt could no longer justify purchasing his favored whisky brand, choosing instead a far cheaper blended malt to satisfy his needs.

The alcohol had the desired effect, dulling the pain and loathing he felt, whilst also allowing him to get at least a few hours' undisturbed sleep each night. Unfortunately, six weeks of near constant alcohol abuse had brought Hunt to a point where he had reached a permanent numb sobriety. He gained no real benefit from the drink any more, it merely allowed him to maintain his current condition.

Day by day Hunt relived the events surrounding his final night at The Exodus. Nothing about that night could be recalled with any clarity, it was simply a mass of distorted and jumbled images and emotions. There were only two aspects of that evening that remained crystal clear in his mind. He had killed people. He was a murderer. Worse than that, he had reveled in their deaths. Hunt could remember the near ecstasy he had felt as the stolen life energy had entered his being and, every time he recalled that feeling it left him with a deep sense of loathing and disgust at what he had become.

Then there was the young girl, murdered before his very eyes. He had been powerless to prevent her death. Her features were etched into his mind, mocking him with their simple purity. He had wanted so much to bring her back as he had been brought back, but that had been beyond his abilities. Each time he tried to sleep he saw her, lying peacefully on that cold, hard, wooden slab, the ugly red stain around her chest where the knife had so cruelly torn her heart asunder, and he wept.

Hunt had been repeatedly told that he was somehow unique, special, that he had some great purpose. He didn't see it. What kind of purpose would require him to kill in order to ensure his own survival? How special was he that he could now take life on a whim, yet could not restore it with the same degree of ease? He was a monster, an executioner, plain and simple. Whatever grand design Andrew had in mind, Hunt wanted no part in it.

Even through the alcohol induced haze, these thoughts had plagued Hunt. They had dogged his every step as he had meandered aimlessly across the countryside. No matter how he processed everything that had happened to him, he kept coming back to the same question. What should he do now?

As he walked through the Parade Gardens, a small park that lay alongside the river Avon which ran through the center of Bath itself, Hunt considered this question once more. He was honest enough to be able to admit that he was running away, from a past that he could not face but also, from a future that he dared not contemplate.

The sun had completely disappeared, leaving just a dark, ruddy glow, peering over the chimney stacks of the old buildings in the town center. Hunt found himself standing in the tree line at the edge of the river itself. He was looking across the river towards a recreational park that lay opposite. Ordinarily Hunt suspected the park would have been used by the general public for ball games, dog walking and the like, this was not the case today however. A circus tent currently stood in the center of the triangular field, itself ringed by a number of caravans and two large, articulated lorries all arranged in an almost protective circle around the blue and yellow striped tent.

In all his life hunt had never before seen a real, live circus. He watched with interest as a show appeared to have drawn to a close. The audience was streaming out of the tent in a long, disordered line. He could hear the shouting and screams from excited children as they re-enacted favorite moments from the performance for their parents. Even before it was completely emptied workmen were gathering around the tent, obviously preparing to dismantle it. Hunt watched in fascination as a man suddenly appeared on the roof of the tent, where he had come from Hunt had could not say. The man sauntered casually across the apex bar that connected the two main poles of the tent, seemingly oblivious to the fact that he was over thirty feet off the ground.

So engrossed was Hunt in the activities across the river that he failed to notice the approach of three figures from behind. A soft crunch of gravel was his first warning that he was not alone. He turned sharply, finding himself faced with three youths. He estimated their age to be around sixteen. They were spaced out in a half circle around him, their posture aggressive. Hunt glanced quickly around and saw that they were alone, the park had emptied rapidly with the coming darkness.

"Hand it over!" The centermost youth demanded gruffly, indicating the heavy-looking bag Hunt had slung across his left shoulder.

Hunt glanced at each in turn. They were all dressed in a similar fashion, dark tracksuit trousers and black hoodies that partially obscured their faces. He guessed they were part of some local street gang and, unwittingly, he had strayed onto their turf. Still, they were barely more than children and he wasn't in the mood for their games.

"Get out of here kids, before one of you gets hurt." He said dismissively, turning away from them.

"Fuck you!" The boy to his left suddenly shouted, launching himself towards Hunts' back.

Despite his dismissiveness, Hunt was prepared for an attack. As the boy landed on his back, arms snaking around Hunts' throat, he dropped suddenly to one knee, whilst pulling hard on the boys arm and bending forwards. This was all that was needed. With a startled cry, the boy flew over Hunts' head, hitting the grassy riverbank with a satisfying thud that knocked the wind out of him. As Hunt rose, turning to face the two remaining attackers they both cannoned into him, sending him sprawling to the ground. One of the boys landed on his chest and instantly began raining blows down upon his head and neck, while his companion set about stripping the bag away from Hunts' unresisting hands.

Hunt used his free arm to protect his face from the flurry of blows, all the while bucking his body upwards in an effort to dislodge his assailant. This would have eventually worked however the first attacker had recovered enough to enter the fray once more. Picking up a loose rock from the rivers' edge he ran up to assist his companion. As soon as he was within reach he swung his arm with all of his might, striking Hunt on the back of his head. There was a satisfying crack of splintering bone and Hunts' arms dropped to his side, limp and useless.

The three boys stood in stunned silence. The youth who had struck Hunt backed away slowly towards the river, the large rock slipping from his shocked hands.

"Is he dead?" He asked in a whisper.

The youth sitting astride Hunts' unmoving chest nodded somberly. He rubbed at the knuckles of his right hand, made sore from the pounding he had just delivered.

"I think so, yeh."

"Shit!" The third youth said. He hoisted Hunts' bag onto his shoulder. "We'd better get out of here."

"In a minute." The young pugilist said, reaching for Hunts' left hand.

"What the fuck are you doing?" His companion with the bag asked. "We've got to go!"

"These gloves look expensive."

"Are you mad?" The bag boy asked incredulously.

By now the left hand glove had been removed and the youth was leaning across towards the right hand.

Without warning Hunt opened his eyes. His sunglasses had fallen off during the struggle and now lay somewhere, unnoticed on the river bank. The youths had been too focused on subduing Hunt to notice the discrepancy in his appearance, until now that is.

The injury Hunt had sustained would have proven lethal to any normal person, for Hunt however it only served as a painful reminder of how much he had changed. As had happened previously in the Club Exodus, Hunts' body was damaged and desperately needed to repair itself. All conscious thought was pushed aside allowing pure instinct to take control. He needed energy. He needed to feed.

It may only have been a trick of the newly rising moonlight but, as Hunts' eyes opened, all three of his assailants were immediately drawn to the disturbing glow that seemed to emanate from the clear right orbit. Two of the boys backed away in opposite directions, one further into the river while the second edged deeper into the shadows of the trees.

Their companion however, never got a chance to react as Hunts' left hand suddenly shot out, grabbing him painfully by the throat. The instant their skin connected, Hunts' power took over. The boy opened his mouth in a silent scream, his hands briefly clawing at Hunt's arm as the life energy left him.

The doomed boys' companions watched in horror as their friend died before their eyes. This was so far beyond anything they had experienced in their short lives that they were rooted to the spot in terror. Having consumed all that the boy had to offer, Hunt tossed the greyed corpse to one side and stood in a low crouch. His wound was healing thanks to the stolen energy, but he needed more.

He turned towards the boy in the trees. The effect of that eerily glowing right eye was like a jolt of electricity. In a split second the boy rose up onto the balls of his feet, turned and ran, discarding the bag he had just stolen in his haste. His belongings were of no interest to Hunt however. He turned slowly to face the remaining youth, who now stood knee deep in the swirling river.

With a cry of animalistic rage Hunt charged towards the terrified teenager. The boy tried to back away, deeper into the murky waters, but he lost his footing on the slippery rocks and mud of the river bed. He tumbled backwards, arms flailing wildly. Without a pause Hunt dived after his quarry, the two of them disappearing beneath the dark, moon drenched waters.

27 | Fool In The Ring

Chapter 2

There was no telling how long Hunt had remained under water. He surfaced only ten feet from the opposite bank, the greyed out corpse of his latest victim surfacing just a few feet away to be carried off downstream. Hunt watched in sullen silence, treading water to maintain position as the body was carried out of sight, then he struck out for the nearest bank.

At this side the river washed up to a low concrete wall, topped with black railings. Hunt grasped the top of the wall and hauled himself out of the water. He sat, dripping water and staring out across the river to the far bank. His injuries had healed once more and his conscious control was restored. What little belongings he had now lay across the river. They may as well have been on the other side of the universe. There was no going back. He couldn't face the gruesome evidence of his recent actions. Two more people were dead at his hands. Young boys that, up until that evening, had an entire life stretched out before them. All of that was gone now. He had taken it all away, and why? So that he could cling on to life just a little bit longer. Hut dropped his head into his hands and wept great, racking sobs that shook his entire body.

He would have been content to remain sat at the river side, lost in grief and self-pity, but the roaring sound of a big diesel engine suddenly assaulted his senses. His attention was drawn back towards the Circus that had first caught his eye. Watching through the tree line that bordered this bank, he could see that the operation to dismantle the tent had progressed well.

A small army of people bustled around the tent performing a variety of tasks. One of the two articulated lorries' had already pulled up alongside the tent, the large double doors of the high-backed trailer standing open as it was being loaded up with spars from the freshly dismantled seating elements. The engine he had just heard was from the second lorry. It was currently disconnected from its trailer and had reversed up to the tent. This vehicle carried a huge generator and winch on the back. Currently a cable from the tent was being attached to the winch.

Hunt headed up the concrete embankment from the waters' edge to the tree line, keeping low and in the shadows. He was considering his options in the wake of the evenings' unexpected activity. He needed to get out of the city before someone stumbled across his handiwork but, having no belongings, no money and no identification Hunt knew that would prove difficult.

The central cupola was being lowered to the ground on two long cables, bringing the rest of the tent down with it. The two cables were attached to hand operated winches located on each of the two king poles. These had to be turned at the same speed in order to bring the cupola down level and straight. Once it was around three meters off the ground, the winching stopped. One of the workers ducked under the tent material to get access to the cupola itself in order to dismantle the rigging for the aerial acts.

Without any warning there was a loud retort, almost like a gunshot. One of the cables flew free and the cupola suddenly dropped to the ground at that free side. A muffled scream issued from within the tent. All work stopped as everyone rushed to rescue their unfortunate colleague.

Hunt was moving before he even realized it. Having seen an opening, an opportunity, he operated now on instinct alone. While everyone's attention was focused elsewhere, Hunt darted across the open field between the tree line and the ring of caravans surrounding what was left of the circus tent. Crouching at the side of one of the caravans, he watched the commotion unfolding around the tent.

It was difficult to determine exactly what was happening, but Hunt surmised that the man from inside the tent had been injured when the cupola fell. Everyone was still gathered in a small group, their attention completely focused away from Hunt.

Moving quickly from the shadowy cover of the caravan, Hunt headed for the passenger side door of the large generator lorry. Easing the door open, he climbed quickly inside, closing the door gently behind him, then tugging sharply on the interior handle to secure the catch in place with the minimum amount of noise. He moved quickly now, climbing over the passenger seat and into a raised compartment which lay beyond a curtain behind the two seats. This was intended to be a small sleeping area for the driver to use on long journeys. Settling onto the small bed, Hunt felt a momentary relief. All he had to do now was to remain undiscovered until after the lorry had left the city.

Hunt had not realized until now, just how exhausted he really was. So far he had been attacked, robbed and beaten. He'd had his skull smashed in, then, much to the surprise of his assailants had recovered enough to kill two of them and chase the third off. Following that he'd swam a river, taken a brusque jog across a park and, finally, stowed away in the cab of an unknown circus lorry. Quite an evenings' work by anyone's standards.

All Hunt wanted was to disappear into the background of the world and lead a nice, quiet, unassuming life. It was starting to look like that would be an unachievable goal. His life just seemed to get more and more complicated with every step.

Despite his best efforts, the physical and emotional toll of the past few hours proved to be simply too much. Hunt actually fell asleep. It was a knack he had developed during his previous life as a war correspondent. There had been many occasions when he had found himself shadowing a military unit across dangerous territory in some unheard of place. In those situations rest was a precious commodity and one learned to take full advantage of every moment that was offered, no matter the surroundings.

The sound of the big diesel engine coughing and spluttering into action startled Hunt out of a surprisingly dreamless slumber. He experienced a fleeting moment of disorientation as his eyes opened to unfamiliar surroundings, then, he remembered. Moving as little as possible, Hunt repositioned himself so he could see through a slight crack in the curtains. The vehicle suddenly lurched backwards, almost tossing him out of the bed and into the back of the seats. He just managed to catch himself in time. There was a heavy thunk and a loud scrape of metal against metal. Hunt surmised that the vehicle had just hitched itself to a trailer.

It seemed that Hunt had timed things just right. Wherever the circus was playing next, they were headed there that night. As if in confirmation, the truck rolled forwards, slowly at first and in a tight circle for a short time before straightening and picking up speed.

Hunt took the opportunity to appraise the driver as he manhandled the huge behemoth through the narrow streets of Bath, shifting up and down through the multiple gear changes with obvious skill. Even seated, the driver did not appear to be very tall, around five feet four or five inches, Hunt guessed. He was also not particularly muscular, more wiry than overtly strong. His black hair was relatively short, but its cut was uneven suggesting it had not been professionally done, and his face exhibited about two days' worth of dark stubble. He was dressed casually in jeans, t-shirt and a lightweight cream colored jacket.

Hunt had no idea what direction they were travelling in, but it was not long before the road seemed to straighten and he could feel the lorry picking up speed so he guessed they had reached some sort of main "A" road.

"I think it's about time you came forward and took a seat neighbor." The driver said casually, a slight nasal quality to his voice.

Hunt did not respond. He had not expected to be caught so soon in the journey.

"Come on pal." The driver insisted, then, almost as an afterthought. "Oh, and if you're thinking of doing anything stupid, this is probably a good time to mention the fact that we are now on the A36, travelling at sixty miles an hour and hauling several tons worth of trailer, metal poles and circus tent, so it's probably not a good idea to get me too excited."

The driver delivered this statement in such a matter of fact way that Hunt couldn't help but smile. With a shrug he decided he may as well comply with the drivers' request. The little man cast a brief, sidelong glance in Hunts' direction as he clambered out from behind the curtain and into the passenger seat in the cab, before turning his attention back to the demands of the road.

"You know, it's customary when you hitch a ride, that you ask the driver permission first."

"You were a bit busy at the time." Hunt quipped, "I didn't want to bother you."

"Hmph." The driver grunted. Hunt noted a slight twitch at the corners of his mouth, as if he were fighting to hold back a smile. "So, what do I call you?"

"Joe." Hunt lied quickly, drawing on the first name that came into his head.

"Well Joe." The driver accepted without question. "I'm Craig, and I'm heading to Eastbourne, so how far do you want to go?"

Hunt did not answer verbally; he simply maintained a fixed stare, his own mouth curling slightly at the corners in a tight smile. Craig registered the look and nodded in easy acceptance.

"Fair enough." He conceded. "Eastbourne it is then."

37 | Fool In The Ring

Chapter 3

It was just past eight o'clock the following morning when the sleek, silver vehicle shot through the sleepy town of Tetbury, heading south. As it hit the early morning traffic the expensive vehicle was forced to slow, dropping gears quickly to accommodate the sudden change in speed. Although English built, the Mercedes-Benz SLR McLaren was not a common sight, and its fine lines and growling engine certainly drew the eyes of the early morning commuters.

A set of traffic lights had forced the beast to a reluctant halt and now it sat, idling, its' driver tapping impatiently on the steering wheel. As much as the car was drawing peoples' attention, that was nothing compared to the admiring glances the driver was attracting. Jane was a striking woman, a raven haired beauty with large, intense brown eyes that were guaranteed to set every male pulse in the vicinity to racing. Any amorous feelings however, would have been severely subdued after one look at her expression. Anger and frustration had molded her normally fine features into a hard, stony mask.

Jane had spent the past six weeks focused on a single task, finding John Hunt. Following events at The Exodus, of which she knew very little, he had simply disappeared. It was clear, after visiting his apartment, that he had packed very little, and Jane had initially assumed that he would only be gone for a couple of days. A week of covert surveillance had been enough to convince her that this was not going to be the case. Hunt had not returned.

The traffic lights changed to green and Jane stomped on the gas pedal. The supercharged V8 engine roared to life, propelling the McLaren away in a cloud of rubber and smoke that turned everyone's heads. It was not long before she had left Tetbury far behind, cruising along the A433 towards Bath at a steady seventy-five miles per hour.

She wasn't worried about the possibility of being stopped by the police. Currently her identification documents declared her to be an Intelligence Agent for MI5, and any background checks would show that she had held this post for the past six years. Her case file stated that she was currently tracking a potential suspect in a terrorist plot involving biological agents, said subject being Mr. John Hunt. This had all been Mantles' idea and, she had to admit, it had worked pretty well so far.

Mantle, acting as her superior within the Agency, had gained access to Hunts' bank and credit card records. This had enabled them to track his movements since leaving Stoke-on-Trent six weeks ago. Hunt obviously had not considered the possibility that anyone might be searching for him and had made no efforts to conceal his movements. His bank card had been used to pay for accommodation on a regular basis, providing an accurate route of travel. Unfortunately due to the erratic nature of the route itself Jane had been unable to determine any end destination. He just seemed to be crisscrossing the country, totally at random, and the best she could do was to maintain a steady pace one day behind him.

Each morning Mantle had called to inform her of where he had spent the previous evening. She would then race to that location in the vain hope of locating him before he moved on again. Admittedly, they weren't catching him, but neither were they losing him completely, until now.

Hunt had purchased accommodation at a small bed and breakfast just outside of Tetbury two days ago. Jane had arrived there yesterday and had stayed at the same place. It was a small, relatively cheap, family run business that could accommodate up to four guests.

All of the rooms were en-suite and Jane had just exited the shower that morning when her phone rang. As expected, it was Mantle. Wrapping a towel around her lithe and muscular form she thumbed the answer key, setting her phone onto the speaker setting and laying it on the dressing table at the foot of the bed.

"Good morning." She said pleasantly, taking a brush to her still damp hair.

"We've got a problem Jane." Mantle answered without preamble.

"Don't tell me we've lost him."

"Oh it's worse than that." Mantle answered. "Do you have a television there?"

"Yes?" Jane answered cautiously.

"Switch it on now! Central news." Mantle ordered.

Obediently, Jane reached for the small remote lying on the bed and flicked the on switch. The small, wall mounted, flat screen television came instantly to life. There were a few moments of rapid button pressing while Jane searched for the relevant channel. Her eyes opened wide in surprise as she was confronted with a full size image of Hunt on the screen before her. It took her a moment to mentally tune into what the off-screen reporter was saying.

"Somerset police have confirmed that they are looking for this man, John Hunt, in connection with the two bodies found this morning ……" Jane hit the mute button. She had heard enough.

"Shit." She said vehemently.

"My thoughts exactly." Mantle said sourly.

"How sure are we that John had anything to do with these bodies?"

"I'm looking at the initial police report now." Mantle answered. "It seems they found a bag containing his wallet and identification at the scene."

"That could mean anything." Jane declared quickly.

"True." Mantle conceded. "The on scene coroners' report is a little harder to dismiss though. Grey corpses, no external wounds or evidence of trauma. Any of that sound familiar Jane?"

"Damn." Jane closed her eyes, shaking her head in disbelief. "What did you do John?" She whispered softly.

"That's what you need to find out Jane." Mantle observed.

"Get down there and put a lid on this, fast. I'm already sending the necessary paperwork over to Somerset police. MI5 will be taking over jurisdiction; you'll be named as the lead investigator. Your first priority is to get this out of the public eye."

"Understood." Jane said firmly. "I'll give you a call once I know more."

As Jane raced towards Bath, she considered the implications of Hunts' actions. She had three main objectives. First and foremost was to pull the media off the case. As much as it had been disturbing to her, seeing Hunts' face broadcast so widely, she knew that this had inadvertently advertised his location to the entire country. There were others out there, less reputable individuals with dubious intent, who were also searching for Hunt. Now they had a starting point to begin looking in earnest.

Then there were the two corpses. Jane knew of Hunts' newly acquired abilities, the world at large however, did not. The sudden appearance of two bodies whose cause of death could not be determined through any scientific method known to man was something to be avoided at all costs. She had to get them removed, along with any examination records that might exist.

The magnitude of both of these tasks was huge, and this was the source of her anger and frustration. All of this could have been avoided were it not for a certain selfish individual who had chosen to go gallivanting around the countryside on their own with not the slightest clue of what he was doing.

This brought Jane to her third task. She could no longer be content with simply following in the mans' wake, she had to find Hunt.

Chapter 4

"Come on Joe, shake it loose." The call was accompanied by three smart bangs on the lorry door.

Hunt opened his eyes, it was light outside. His brain felt like it was stuffed with cotton wool, a sure sign that he needed more sleep. With a slight groan, he squeezed himself out of the small compartment in the back of the lorry, into the passenger seat. Craig was waiting for him outside, he watched with a slight smirk on his face as Hunt climbed down from the cab.

"Not the most comfortable of places are they?" He said knowingly. Hunt shrugged.

"Better than anything I had to look forward to."

"I don't doubt it." Craig accepted. "Come on, the boss wants to see you." Without waiting for a response, Craig turned and headed off in the direction of a medium size caravan stood at one end of the field. Hunt followed close behind.

Little had been said during the night-time drive. Once
Craig had determined that Hunt, or Joe, as he had called himself, posed no threat, he had seemed content. Hunt had expected a barrage of questions, but they never came. Towards the end of the journey Craig had surmised that Hunt had nowhere else to go so had offered the cab for the night, an offer hunt was in no position to refuse.

Having arrived in darkness, Hunt had not had the chance to take in his surroundings. Now as, he followed after Craig, he could see that they were in a large field. The lorry he had slept in was positioned towards the center and, since their arrival, two other caravans had appeared. They were parked towards the edge of the field, forming the beginnings of the ring Hunt had noticed at the previous ground.

As he looked around, Hunt spied a large sign at the entrance, Princes Park. It meant nothing to him. He knew they were close to the sea however, close enough at least to hear the crashing of the waves and taste the salty brine in the air.

Craig led Hunt towards the smaller of the two caravans. It was a single axle, two berth caravan, about five and a half meters in length, predominately white in color with a grey horizontal stripe just above the wheel arch on which were written the words, Abbey Executive. Craig knocked on the single barn door, a woman's voice answered from within.

"It's open Craig." The voice was deep and firm.

Opening the door, Craig motioned for Hunt to enter first. The interior was small and cramped but well-ordered and tidy. A kitchen area was just to the right as Hunt entered, the living space being located to the left. The bed had been folded back into comfortable looking seating benches that covered the two sides of the caravan at that end, a small drop down table standing between them.

Hunt was immediately aware of the woman observing him as he entered. Seated at the small table, her piercing green eyes held him in a steady gaze for several moments before she motioned to the bench opposite.

"Take a seat." She offered.

Hunt took the indicated seat while Craig remained standing, leaning back against the small sink at the other end of the caravan.

"So you're the stray Craig picked up on his way through last night?" It was more a statement than a question.

Hunt nodded silently taking the opportunity to study his host. She was small only in terms of her stature, her physical build was impressive. She wore a tight fitting, black, sleeveless top that showed off her broad, well-muscled shoulders and arms. Her long, curly black hair framed an attractive, but stern face.

"You look like crap!" She said bluntly, a slight smirk on her face.

"It's been a rough night." Hunt answered, she nodded.

"So I gather. So what are your plans now?"

The question surprised Hunt. He hadn't really had the chance to give his situation much thought. Events had moved with surprising speed over the past twelve hours. He no longer had any possessions, money or identification. All that remained of his former life were the clothes on his back, and they were still damp.

"I don't really have any plans." He answered honestly.

"Well, we're looking at being here for the next week and, thanks to a stupid accident last night, we're a man down." She fired a hard look in Craig's direction, he winced slightly. "I can offer you fifty pounds a day, cash, and a roof over your head."

Hunt blinked in surprise. "You're offering me a job? But you don't know anything about me."

"All I need to know is, can you work? It's nothing special, manual labor and it probably won't last beyond the week but, if you want it, it's yours."

Hunt looked across at Craig who shrugged and nodded, grinning slightly. In truth, he wasn't really in a position to refuse.

"Sure, why not?" He said eventually.

"Good." The woman said simply, she turned towards Craig. "Take him over to your place. You've probably got an hour or so before everyone starts arriving. Plenty of time to get him fed, watered and cleaned up a bit."

"Sure thing boss." Craig said merrily. "Come on Joe, let's get you some breakfast."

As Hunt stood he looked down at the woman. "Thank you." He said simply. She inclined her head in silent response and watched him leave.

Craig's caravan was substantially larger than the one he had just left. Easily three times as long and sitting on twin axels, it looked quite impressive to Hunts' untrained eye. There was a slim woman busily erecting an awning off the side of the caravan, she turned towards them as they approached.

"Haven't you got that up yet?" Craig called out, his face beaming. She smiled easily, brown eyes twinkling mischievously.

"I don't see you doing a lot you lazy sod!" She bantered back before turning to Hunt. "You must be Joe, I'm Sarah." She extended her hand in greeting.

Hunt looked warily down, noting her delicate fingers. He suddenly felt uncomfortable and a little embarrassed. He didn't want to seem impolite or awkward but, at the same time, he couldn't trust himself to shake her hand without gloves.

"I...I'm sorry." He stammered. "I have a problem with physical contact, O.C.D." He lied. It was the first thing that came to mind, but it seemed to suffice.

Sarah's smile never wavered as she withdrew the offered hand.

"Don't worry about it honey." She said. "Craig wasn't kidding though, you are a mess. Get yourself inside. The bedroom is on the right. I've laid out a dressing gown for you."

Hunt paused, the confusion evident on his face. Both Sarah and Craig laughed a little.

"Those clothes need washing." Sarah explained. "I can't very well do that while you're still in them now, can I?"

Hunt smiled a little sheepishly. With a mumbled thanks he headed into the caravan, wondering all the while what he was letting himself in for.

Fool In The Ring

Chapter 5

Detective Inspector Cunningham was not a happy man. What had started out as an interesting and potentially rewarding day had rapidly turned into one of the most frustrating days of his professional life so far.

Cunningham was a career police officer who had worked himself up through the ranks with intelligence, diligence and integrity. At forty-five he had, so far, managed to prevent the ravages of time from leaving too great a mark on his appearance. His full head of black hair was only slightly greying at the temples while his green eyes still retained the sparkle of youth. Although not particularly vain, he did still work out just enough to keep the middle aged spread at bay, allowing him to continue wearing the smart, three piece suits which were his passion.

He had been one of the first to receive the call when the body had been discovered on the river bank in Parade Gardens. By the time he had reached the scene, one body had
turned into two. The second had turned up tangled in the branches of a tree that had fallen into the river just around the next bend. It did not take a genius to work out that the two bodies were connected in some way. Even without a cause of death, the visual aspects of the corpses were just too alike to be ignored, or dismissed as a coincidence. The coroner was baffled, and that didn't happen very often. At first glance this had all the hallmarks of a fascinating case. Unfortunately it was a case he was no longer allowed to pursue, hence his frustration.

It began an hour ago with a phone call from his Superintendent instructing him in no uncertain terms to cease all further investigations. It seemed that their chief suspect, Mr. John Hunt, was a person of interest to MI5 and they were taking over the investigation.

This was not a situation Cunningham had ever encountered before. Yes, he had had previous dealings with MI5 with regard to domestic terrorism cases but, always before, they had taken an advisory role. He could only surmise that, if they were taking over completely, then Mr. Hunt must be a serious player, but, if that were the case, then why had he never come up on anyone's radar before now? It didn't make sense, and Cunningham liked things to make sense, it was almost a requirement of his job.

Now D.I. Cunningham was relegated to the role of security guard, maintaining the integrity of the crime scene in order to pass it over to the agent MI5 had dispatched. His colleague, meanwhile, was at the other end of the city where the mortuary was located. He had the unenviable task of ensuring that the two bodies, and all applicable evidence the
Scenes of Crime Officers had so far collected, was made ready for the rest of the team from MI5 to collect. This had to be organized in a very specific and precise manner in order to maintain the chain of evidence. Cunningham winced as he thought about the amount of paperwork todays' events were going to

generate. He was likely to be chained to his desk for the remainder of the week thanks to this mess, and that was not how he preferred to operate.

Cunningham was so lost in his grumbling assessment of the repercussions he expected to face that he failed to notice Jane approaching his position from the main road that passed the far side of the park. It was only at the point where she ducked agilely under the crime scene tape, that he became aware of her presence.

"Excuse me Miss!" He called urgently, walking quickly towards her.

"D'Arcy. MI5." She said abruptly, producing a small leather wallet from her jacket and flipping it open to reveal her identification.

"Oh." Cunningham said in surprise.

This was not what he had been expecting. He studied her as she approached. Young, attractive, professionally dressed in a well-tailored, black trouser suit, a white blouse and sensible shoes, she definitely did not fit his image of how a government agent should look. He turned to follow her as she breezed past him towards the center of the crime scene.

"I'm …"

"Detective Inspector Cunningham." She cut him off abruptly. "I know." She stopped suddenly and turned back to him. "Are you coming?"

She may not have looked like a government agent but there was no mistaking that arrogant, imperious bearing. Cunningham mumbled an apology and fell into step alongside her as they continued on to the crime scene proper.

"So, tell me what you have." Jane ordered.

"You've read the reports?"

"On the way over." She confirmed.

"Then I don't know what you need me for." Cunningham stated petulantly.

"D.I. Cunningham, you have over twenty years on the force. By all accounts, you are a savvy, astute investigator, so do me a favor. Drop the attitude and give me the benefit of your knowledge and experience." The rebuke was delivered in a flat, emotionless tone.

Cunningham found himself rapidly reassessing his previous assumptions regarding Agent D'Arcy. Despite her obvious youth she was firm, authoritative, almost aggressive, yet there was no hint of ego about her. Surprisingly,

Cunningham found himself to be quite impressed with her.

"Fair enough." He acceded.

By now they had reached the point where the first body had been found. Jane was crouching down on the balls of her feet, examining the area intently, trying to picture the sequence of events that had taken place.

"Tell me about the victims." She ordered softly.

Cunningham produced a notebook from an inside pocket of his suit jacket. He began flipping back and forth through its pages.

"Paul Griffiths and Adrian Marshall, victims one and two respectively. Both teenage boys aged sixteen, both runaways from a local children's home and both members of the same street gang."

"No families?" Jane asked.

"None that we know of." Cunningham confirmed. "They'd both been in the system virtually since birth."

Cunningham evidenced some sympathy for the two victims but, for Jane, this was the best news he could have given her. No families meant there was no-one around to apply pressure on the police to solve the boys' murders. One less thing to clean up.

"So what do you think happened here?" She asked.

"It has all the hallmarks of a mugging gone bad." Cunningham answered.

"Go on." Jane pressed.

"Well, " Cunningham continued slowly, mentally creating a sequence in his head that would fit the evidence. "Your man Hunt was wandering around here late at night and the boys saw an opportunity for an easy take down. They jumped him, fought and one of them hit him with a rock."

"Why do you say that?" Jane asked.

"We recovered a blood soaked rock from the scene and there was a substantial pool of it on the grass. Since neither of the victims showed any external signs of an injury that could have produced that level of blood loss, it's a reasonable bet the blood belongs to Hunt."

"Okay. So what next?"

"That's where it gets a bit tricky." Cunningham admitted. "Cause of death for both victims is unclear. We know that Griffiths died here, while

Marshall made it to the river. We've got a blood spatter trail leading to the waters' edge as well so it's a good bet that Hunt chased Marshall into the water. Marshall got caught up in the trees a little way down, maybe Hunt didn't. I'd say it's even money he washes up further down river."

"You think he's dead as well?"

"I wouldn't be surprised." Cunningham admitted.

Jane was impressed. In all but two particulars, she figured Cunningham had pieced together an accurate sequence of events. He hadn't mentioned a third assailant however. From the footprints around the scene Jane felt sure there was a third man, or boy, one who survived and managed to get away. The other fault in the Inspectors reasoning concerned Hunt himself. Jane knew of his abilities and, therefore, knew the cause of death for the two unfortunate teenagers. She didn't believe for a minute that Hunt had simply died in the river and been washed downstream like some piece of errant flotsam.

Jane stood slowly, staring out across the river towards the far bank as she considered possible alternatives. Her gaze took in the recreational grounds on the opposite bank. A small white transit with a long, twenty-four foot caravan in tow was just pulling off the grass, heading for the main road. Gypsies?

"What's going on there?" She asked, pointing towards the departing caravan.

"Oh, there was a circus there last night." Cunningham informed her. "It was their last day yesterday. Most of them
had already left by the time we arrived this morning. I had some PCSO's over there, questioning the ones that were still around but, they didn't see anything. It seems they had a fairly major accident with their tent last night, put one of them in the hospital."

"Interesting." Jane murmured. She turned abruptly and started to walk back towards the main road. "Thank you Detective Inspector," She called without looking back. "You've been very helpful."

"What? Is that it?"

"If I need anything more, I know where to find you."

He was dismissed, that was how it felt at least. His shoulders slumped a little dejectedly.

"I can hardly wait." He muttered caustically, watching her rapidly diminishing back.

For her part, Jane had no intention of contacting the Detective Inspector ever again. She had everything she needed now. The real question was, what would she do with it?

She had parked her car just across from the gardens. Reaching it, she climbed in and immediately began making a call from her mobile. It was answered on the third ring.

"Mantle." Came the gruff voice at the other end.

"It's definitely Hunt." Jane stated without preamble. She then went on to outline the events as Cunningham had described them to her, adding her own observations regarding the third boy and Hunts survival prospects. There were a few moments silence once she had finished while Mantle assessed the information.

"So, there's a living witness?" He said eventually.

"It would seem so." Jane confirmed sourly. "That's a loose end we can't afford."

"I agree. Do you have any way to find this third man?" Mantle asked.

"I think so." Jane answered. "It'll probably take a couple of days though, so you'll have to chase down the Circus."

"You really think he left with them?" Mantle asked dubiously.

"It fits." Jane answered simply. "He needed a way to get out of dodge without being seen. At the moment that seems the likeliest candidate to me."

"If you say so." Mantle still wasn't entirely convinced, but he had come to trust Jane's instincts over the years. "What did you say they were called again?"

"Circus Starburst."

"Very well Jane. You go chase after the boy and I'll find the Circus. I'll send you the details once I track them down, and you can meet me there when you're done."

"Understood."

Jane thumbed the end button on her phone and tossed it onto the passenger seat. She sat for a moment, her face a grim, determined mask. There was a third witness, she knew it. Right now she had only one lead to go on. She had to go and find his gang.

As the big McLaren engine roared into life, catapulting her away from the curbside, Jane failed to notice a somewhat non-descript dark blue Ford pulling away and falling into traffic just a few cars behind.

Chapter 6

As he stepped out of Craig's caravan, Hunt felt refreshed. Craig and Sarah had taken great pains over his welfare. While his clothes were being laundered, Sarah had cooked an excellent breakfast, a British classic consisting of crispy bacon, thick, juicy sausages, eggs, beans and toast, all washed down with copious amounts of strong tea. Hunt hadn't eaten this well since first leaving his home town over a month ago.

Sarah kept Hunt company while he ate, filling him full of information about the Circus and how everything worked.

"Angela's the boss." Sarah had said, meaning the lady he had met earlier that morning. "My

Craig is the Tent Master, between them, they run the whole show."

"What about you?" Hunt had asked.

"I help Angela out with some of the administration and, during the shows, I'll work one of the concession stalls."

From what Hunt could gather, the Circus was a very tight-knit community where everyone had their assigned roles. Most people multi-tasked, usually fulfilling two or more roles. Artists would double up as laborers, while spouses would generally take on the less physical roles, driving, operating the concession stands, or tidying up after the shows.

"So what happened to your face?" Sarah had asked quite bluntly at one point during their conversation.

"I was injured in a fire." Hunt answered. It wasn't exactly a lie, but neither was it exactly the truth. Sarah accepted the answer at face value without further probing. "You're the first person to ask me." Hunt noted.

"We don't usually get into other peoples' business." Sarah responded. "You'll get used to it. The show tends to attract people who don't really fit in anywhere else. We don't ask a lot of questions. We don't judge. So long as everyone does the job they're here to do then that's all that really matters to us."

Hunt found the attitude refreshing. He certainly fit into the category as a misfit now, and the idea of gaining acceptance somewhere had a definite appeal. Unfortunately his natural cynicism kicked in at that point. He had already been accepted once since the accident that had so radically changed him, and that experience had not turned out very well. Could he really put himself in that position again?

Sarah noted the change in Hunts' expression, how his eyes became distant and guarded. It was clear that she wanted to say something, but the sudden reappearance of Craig, breezing brightly into the caravan stopped her.

"Here you go Joe." Craig said, cheerfully placing a carrier bag on the table in front of Hunt.

Craig had disappeared earlier while Hunt was eating. He
had said something about having a few errands to run. As Hunt looked through the contents of the bag he understood what those errands were.

Rummaging through the bag, he found a pair of steel black, toe-capped boots, a pair of sand colored leather work gloves and sunglasses. He looked up at Craig's smiling face, a questioning expression furrowing his brows.

"I couldn't have you working on the tent without some form of protection mate." Craig clarified.

"And the sunglasses?"

"Angela suggested it. She figured you'd feel more comfortable in them. In truth I reckon she thought you'd put the punters off, giving them the evil eye, so to speak."

"Craig!" Sarah said in a shocked voice, slapping him on the arm.

Hunt smiled good naturedly. He was surprised, and more than a little humbled, by the generosity being displayed by these people who barely knew him. He didn't really know how to respond.

"Don't worry Joe." Craig said in apparent understanding. "Consider it a down payment. You can pay me back at the end of the week, assuming you plan on earning your keep."

That was a not so subtle hint that it was time to go to work. The next few hours were an education for Hunt. He had never before considered the level of complexity associated with the construction of a circus tent.

The long, flat-bed trailer they had brought in the previous evening formed the center point around which the tent was built. Craig began walking a wide circle around this holding a spray can filled with white paint, periodically he would stop and paint a cross on the ground. Hunt followed closely behind, unloading heavy, four foot, metal stakes from one of the storage compartments on the trailer and laying one on each cross. There were over eighty in total.

As they were doing this, the rest of the crew began to arrive. Cars and caravans of all sizes drew onto the field and began taking up positions around the tent area, forming a compact ring. Everyone seemed to know where they were going and, with little fuss the caravans were parked up, unhitched and made ready in a very short space of time.

Once settled, the crew began appearing around the tent trailer, preparing to join in. Craig handled the introductions and Hunt was suddenly faced with a continuous blur of names and hand shaking. He knew he would never remember them all at once, but that didn't seem to matter. All that was important right now was raising the tent.

With the stakes laid out, the two center poles came next. They were known as King poles, a name which Hunt considered to be highly appropriate as they were massive looking square steel structures, designed to support the entire weight of the tent. It took every man there to lift them off the back of the flat-bed and position them ready for raising, a job which was performed by the mechanical winch on the back of the generator lorry.

The center section of the tent, or Cupola, as it was known, was a triangular steel, lattice framework, and attached to the king poles via long steel cables. The tent itself was a durable plastic, several millimeters thick and was effectively draped
over the Cupola. As the Cupola was winched off the trailer using the hand operated winches on the King Pole, the tent rose naturally with it.

The huge swathe of blue and yellow striped plastic rose majestically skywards. It was an impressive sight, but not one on which Hunt had much time to dwell as there were still a multitude of tasks to complete.

It was a long day of hard labor, Hunt couldn't remember a time when he had worked so hard, but it had felt good. There was something almost pure about the mindless expenditure of physical energy towards a shared goal. Despite the wide and varied mix of characters among the crew, they all seemed to work together with a surprising degree of cohesiveness.

By about three in the afternoon the work was completed, the tent was up. The interior had been laid out with a central ring, three large raised banks of seating and a small, triangular shaped back stage area for the performers and their props. Hunt sat down on the front seating bank, wiping sweat off his brow while looking around in almost child-like wonder. Craig came over with two cups of tea, handing one to hunt as he took a seat himself.

"So what do you think Joe?" Craig asked.

"It's tougher than I expected." Hunt admitted, Craig laughed.

"You've got it easy pal. We had no shows today, so we could take our time."

"You're kidding, right." Hunt asked, genuinely shocked.

"I wish." Craig answered, taking a sip of the steaming tea. "Normally we'd have started work at about seven in the morning. We'd get the tent up, do a lunchtime and evening show, then pull her back down, load her up and move off to the next ground."

"Jesus, that sounds pretty intense." Hunt could barely believe the level of effort involved in maintaining that kind of physical routine. As it was, he felt like every muscle in his body was queuing up to complain.

"It's worse for the performers." Craig conceded. "They barely get a break on days like that."

"So how come you're not doing that this week then?"

"We were supposed to be doing a two day stand just outside of Portsmouth before coming here." Craig confessed. "They pulled us at the last minute, some problem with the local residents. Angela managed to get the ground permit here extended but we didn't have the time to get the performance license extended as well"

"That's a bit rough." Hunt observed

"It happens." Craig responded philosophically. "It's not so bad really. It gives us all a chance to catch our breath a little, plus I get some time to do a little maintenance."

"So what happens next today then?"

"For you? Not a lot really. You can pretty much do what you want for the rest of the day. There's going to be a bit of a barbeque tonight though, outside mine. It'll be a good chance for you to really get to know people."

"Oh, ok." Hunt was not sure about mixing too much with people on a social level. As welcoming as everyone had been so far, he still didn't feel like he really belonged.

"Oh, I nearly forgot. We don't have any space in the
caravans right now so I'm afraid you'll have to put up with my cab again tonight, but you won't have to worry about food, me and Sarah will look after you on that score."

"That's really good of you." Hunt said sincerely.

"No problem pal." Craig responded, flashing Hunt his now familiar smile.

Chapter 7

Despite it being the last week of August and the seasons turning evermore towards autumn, the afternoon sun remained warm. Hunt was thankful for the gentle, cooling breeze blowing in from the sea as he left the circus ground. He had decided that he needed some time alone, time to think.

He headed for the cool ocean that lay barely a stones' throw away. Dodging traffic, Hunt crossed the main road, leaving only a short footpath between himself and the golden, sandy beach. The path itself was flanked on the one side by a white faced, four story block of flats, while on the other was "Fort Fun", a garishly

colored, miniature children's theme park. As Hunt proceeded steadily along the footpath, oblivious to the screams and shouts of over excited children from his right, his attention was drawn to one of the long apartment balconies. Looking up he saw a youngish looking woman standing at the balcony rail. She was thin and petite but well-proportioned and shapely, a fact made more apparent by the
flimsy looking bikini and brightly colored sarong style skirt that she wore. She appeared to be watching his every step. At any other time, Hunt may well have approached her, but not today. Company was the last thing on his mind at that moment. Shaking his head, he turned away and continued on towards the beach.

A well maintained, concrete pathway ran east-west along the coastline. Hunt chose to walk along this rather than on the beach itself. He was physically tired, and the act of trudging through the soft, golden sand would have been too much for his weary body. Heading east, towards the marina, Hunt maintained a steady pace, allowing the constant whispering of the cool waters to his right to lull his senses. They seemed to caress the coastline with a steady, gentle rhythm that he found somehow comforting.

Looking back at the events of the past year, Hunt despaired at the extent to which his life had changed. Somehow, the presence of the sandy beach sent his mind back to another time and place, a place full of sand and smoke, and noise of a very different sort. The explosion, that single, random moment, had been the point where his life had irrevocably changed.

The question Hunt suddenly found himself asking was, how random was that explosion? He should have died, did in fact die, twice, yet, somehow, he came back, he survived. Was that pure chance or was there already a design at work? He had no way to answer that question, and that bothered him.

Since his return to the world, he had been faced with one extraordinary occurrence after another. He had witnessed
things he could not explain, had done things he would never have believed possible. Recalling the events at the Exodus, the image of Eve suddenly formed in his mind. Even knowing she was dead, that image still retained the power to set his pulse racing, his breath catching

momentarily in his chest. The moment was fleeting however. She was dead, he had killed her.

This was the biggest change of all. Hunt was a murderer. It seemed that his continued survival required the destruction of others. Five people had died in the Exodus, four of them by his hand. This fact alone was soul destroying. What made it worse, however, was the knowledge that he had not merely killed them, he had fed upon them. He had stolen their life energy in order to replenish his own and repair his shattered body. The very fact that he had this power was difficult to comprehend. This was the reason he had chosen to leave Andrew outside the Exodus.

Hunt had never been a believer in magic, religion or the paranormal, considering them to be nothing more than social constructs designed to shore up the minds of weak individuals, allowing them to function in a world they barely understood.

Now he was in the position of not only believing in, but also trying to control, a power he could barely comprehend. Faced with such a daunting and terrifying prospect, his mind had retreated, and he had fled. Leaving behind The Exodus, Andrew and whatever great purpose he referred to, Hunt had run off into the night, hoping desperately, that he could lose himself in obscurity.

The events of the past twenty-four hours had proven to Hunt that his hopes were in vain. Running had gained him
nothing but further pain. The body count had now risen to six and Hunt had no expectations that it would end there. Was he destined to leave a trail of destruction and death wherever he went? Was his continued existence to be dependent upon the lives of others? Why had he been given this terrible power? What grand purpose did it serve? These were the questions that plagued his consciousness as his steps led him towards Sovereign Harbor.

Two great man-made, stone walls marked the entrance to the harbor, one straight, the other curved, giving the impression of some huge, grey, asymmetrical claw. These structures served to protect the harbor from the ravages of an unmerciful sea and encroaching tides. Hunt found a spot midway along the straight wall where he could sit and think, heedless of the salt water splashing across him, driven by the gradually rising sea breeze.

Chapter 8

The Sun was just dropping below the horizon, casting dusky red shadows across the streets as Mantle pulled his olive-colored F-type Jaguar off the A3 and onto the A27, heading towards Havant on the outskirts of Portsmouth. The growling, V6 engine protested at being forced into a more sedate pace as the impressive coupe traversed ever more populated roads.

It had taken Mantle most of the day to determine the location of Circus Starburst's next performance. Now as he neared his final destination, he fervently hoped that Janes' instincts would be proven correct.

Unlike Jane, Mantle held some degree of sympathy for Hunt. He knew that allowing Hunt to wander off on his own was a mistake, but, he also felt he understood why Hunt had made that choice. Still, understanding and sympathy aside, the man had made an absolute mess of things, and a very loud and public mess at that. This was not a situation that could be allowed to continue.

It was then with some degree of dismay, and no small amount of frustration that Mantle turned off the main street, heading North towards Havant Park. The Park was several hundred yards ahead and, even from this distance, it was abundantly clear, there was no circus tent in sight.

As Mantle approached the park he noticed a small, diner just off the road near the entrance. It still appeared to be open so, on impulse Mantle swung the sleek machine into one of the vacant parking spaces nearby.

Exiting the vehicle, he stood for a few moments, surveying the area. The steady drone of traffic from the nearby streets went completely unnoticed as his focus was drawn entirely to the empty field on the far side of the diner. No circus tent, no caravans, no vehicles of any description. Not a single indication of a circus ever having been there. With a heavy sigh, Mantle headed towards the diner.

It was clear that had he been a few minutes later then the diner would have been closed. Chairs were resting on the tables and the place was empty of people save for two women. One, young girl, probably around seventeen was busily mopping the floor while the second, older woman was occupied at the cash register, obviously counting out the days takings. She looked up as Mantle entered.

"Sorry sweetie." She said in a friendly, cheerful voice. "We're just about to close up."

"That's all right." Mantle answered quickly walking purposefully over towards her while taking care to dodge the madly whipping mop that was rapidly approaching. "I wasn't really looking for food." The middle aged woman looked up from her counting, a quizzical expression on her face.

"Actually." Mantle pressed on quickly. "I was wondering if you might be able to help me. I was told there was a circus performing here tonight. You wouldn't happen to know anything about that would you?"

"Yes. The council pulled the plug on them only yesterday."

"Really? Why?"

"Oh, we had some trouble with the circus folk a couple of years back. The residents around here decided they didn't want them back again. They've been protesting about it for weeks now. I guess they finally won. Shame really. I never had any problem with them and they were always good customers for me here."

"You wouldn't happen to know where they will have gone now, would you?"

"Actually, I do. Their advance team were having breakfast here yesterday morning when the Council reps came and told them to move off. I heard them talking about moving straight on to their next ground over in Eastbourne."

"You wouldn't know where in Eastbourne?" Mantle pressed.

The woman smiled as she reached under the counter by the cash register. She pulled out a large piece of rolled up gloss paper which she handed to Mantle. As he unrolled it, he realized it was a very gaudy, vibrant advertising poster.

"May I keep this?" He asked.

"Of course you can." The woman answered simply. "I've got another one here. My son loves the circus so I always try and get him a poster whenever one comes through."

"Thank you very much" Mantle said sincerely.

Exiting the diner Mantle almost ran back to his vehicle. Once inside he started the engine then leaned back into his seat, letting the purr of the idling beast relax his mind as he considered his options. He reached decisively for his phone, hitting the first number on speed dial then transferring to the cars built in hands free system.

The call connected after only a few rings.

"You have reached the number of Agent D'Arcy. I am unable to take your call at this time but if you leave your name and number I will return your call as soon as possible."

There was a long tone, then silence.

"Damn it Jane." Mantle said in exasperation. "Call me back as soon as you get this. I have a lead on the Circus." Mantle then proceeded to fill in the details he had learned from the diner. "I'm going to find a place here for the night, then I'll head over to Eastbourne in the morning. Catch up with me there as soon as you can."

Chapter 9

The vibrating phone went unnoticed on the passenger seat of Janes' Mercedes, its screen eventually going dark.

The vehicle itself looked decidedly out of place in its current location, an old, abandoned industrial estate on the eastern edge of Bath. The aged buildings stood precariously, in varying states of disrepair and choked with undergrowth as the land continued the long battle to reclaim its own.

Jane had spent the majority of the day immersed in the seedy underbelly of Baths criminal element, such as it was, searching for the elusive third person who had witnessed the mornings' events which had culminated in the murders of two teenage boys and the disappearance of John Hunt. Finally her search had borne fruit.

According to the information she had gleaned thus far, somewhere amongst the assembled derelicts there resided a thoroughly disreputable fence. By all reports the man in question had modeled himself after Fagin from "Oliver Twist", enlisting young children and teenagers to roam the streets of Bath, procuring items of worth on his behalf.

The two murder victims were both in this mans' employ and it seemed reasonable to assume that the errant third person may well have been as well.

Leaving her vehicle at the outskirts of the industrial estate Jane had proceeded on foot, systematically moving from building to building, searching each in turn for her quarry. So intent was she on her search that Jane failed to notice a car rolling quietly to a stop alongside her Mercedes. It was the same dark-blue Ford that had followed her from the crime scene earlier that morning. Unknown to Jane, the two occupants of the Ford had trailed steadily behind her throughout the course of the day.

Jane had reached a corner of one of the large warehouse buildings. As she peered cautiously around, she was just in time to see a young boy approaching one of the warehouses further ahead. He squeezed through a broken panel to the side of one of the main doorways'. Bingo, she thought, and sprinted quickly across the intervening space as soon as the boy was out of sight.

Rather than follow the boy directly, Jane elected to find another point of access to the building. After a brief search she found a partially open window on the far side of the building. The single glass pane was cracked and smeared with grime and the window itself was hinged at the top. She eased the bottom edge carefully away from the frame, enough that with only a little effort, she could squeeze herself through the gap. Her lithe frame made short work of gaining access and she carefully lowered herself gently to the ground with barely a sound.

Finding herself in one of a number of side rooms which surrounded an empty, dust strewn expanse, she paused briefly to take stock. She could hear the low murmur of voices in the distance. An open doorway led from her room to the main part of the warehouse. Moving towards this now, she pressed her back up against the wall and peered around the side of the frame for a better view.

Even from this vantage point the source of the voices remained hidden. The central floor space in the warehouse was clear, but Jane could see shadows moving in one of the office spaces on the far side. Moving swiftly and silently, Jane crossed the intervening space, bringing herself to rest on the right side of the office door frame. From this new vantage point she could easily hear the conversation being conducted from within the office.

"Not a bad little haul kid." The voice was slightly high pitched, with a wheedling nasal quality. "I can give you fifty quid for the lot."

"Fifty?" This second voice resonated with youth. Jane guessed the owner to be the young boy she had followed into the warehouse. "The watch alone is worth four times that."

"Boy thinks this is a negotiation." Nasal said sarcastically. "It's fifty quid, take it or leave it."

"Fine." The boy answered after a moment's thought.

Jane had decided that she had heard enough. This was clearly the man she was looking for. With barely a qualm she straightened up and boldly stepped into the office, taking two steps forward to move herself clear of the doorway.

"Interesting little operation you have here." She observed calmly, with no small amount of arrogance.

"Who the fuck are you?"

The nasal voice belonged to a little man seated in a rickety wooden chair before a small, equally decrepit looking desk. His short, greasy, dark hair clung to his head like an ill-fitting skull cap. A dark, brittle looking beard clung to the pitted and pock-marked wasteland of his face in uneven clumps. Worn Jeans and an old, threadbare corduroy jacket completed the overall look, which was one of utter destitution.

The boy that Jane had followed stood in front of the desk. He had turned upon her entrance and his eyes widened in fear and surprise. It was, however, the third figure in the room that drew the majority of Jane's attention. A short, brutish-looking skin-head. His well-muscled frame and deep-set, cold eyes easily denoted him as the muscle behind the little weasels' illicit operation.

"You just made a big mistake lady." The weasel noted dangerously. "Alex…"

Without any further prompting the brute stepped forward, his expressionless face fixed on Jane, hands flexing in anticipation.

Jane had hoped to avoid any unpleasantness, one look at the skin-heads' face however, told her that was no longer an option. She sighed deeply.

It wasn't much of a fight. The whole thing was over in a matter of seconds. A stiff-fingered jab to the throat crushed the brutes' windpipe. As he dropped to his knees, fighting for breath Jane followed up with a brutal knee to the face.

There was a moment of stunned silence as the young boy and the weasel starred mutely at the crumpled form of Alex.

Jane turned her attention the boy who had begun to shake with fear.

"You. Leave." She said simply, indicating the doorway with a nod of her head.

The boy needed no further urging. With lightning speed he darted from the room, grateful to have got out unharmed. Jane, meanwhile, turned her penetrating gaze back to the weasel. Instinctively he knew he would not be so fortunate as his rapidly departing employee.

"What do you want?" The weasel asked. His voice had risen almost an octave and quivered slightly in response to the stress of the situation.

Jane stepped forwards, resting her hands on the small desk and leaning forwards menacingly.

"Two of your boys were killed this morning." She stated simply, her voice flat and cold. "But there was a third one there. He got away. I want to know where he is, and I think you can tell me."

Jane had become focused upon her quarry to the exclusion of all else. By the time she heard the soft crunch of loose rubble behind her, she knew, it was already too late. She turned quickly, her body preparing to fight. The blow struck her with incredible force, hitting the side of her head with a dull thud and sending her clear across the table to land in a crumpled heap by the far wall. Darkness rapidly enfolded her in its embrace and the last thing she was aware of as she succumbed to its grip was a rough laugh and a voice that she vaguely recognized.

Chapter 10

It had been a difficult few weeks for Mr. Bera. There had been so much to organize in the wake of Hunts' last visit to "Club Exodus".

With the Flame of Ephesus irrevocably destroyed, Exodus no longer served a purpose. Bera was still unsure how Hunt had managed that particular feat. Worse still was the destruction of Eve. She had woefully underestimated Hunts' abilities, as indeed, had he. Bera growled to himself as he thought about this. Despite her apparent demise Bera remained a loyal servant, and he knew exactly what was required of him now.

Currently he was heading south towards London, his chauffeur driven Limousine rapidly eating up the miles. Close behind a plain white transit van followed. Bera glanced back, checking that the van was still with them. The driver of the van had no clue as to the value of the cargo he was transporting.

Bera was brought back from his silent mental meanderings by the sound of his mobile phone. He reached for it and, after checking the caller I.D., quickly thumbed the answer button.

"I hope you have some good news for me Carl." Bera said without preamble, his tone low and menacing.

He listened patiently for several moments, his stony expression gradually softening, becoming more thoughtful.

"An interesting turn of events." He said finally. "Bring Miss D'Arcy to me Carl, as quick as you can."

He listened again for a moment.

"No Carl. Hunt can wait for now. Bring her. And Carl…" There was a momentary pause, "make sure she is not harmed in any way."

Bera thumbed the disconnect button without waiting for a response. Tossing his phone onto the seat next to him, he leaned back into the plush leather upholstery, allowing a relaxed smile to grace his features.

Chapter 11

It was well past sundown by the time Hunt returned to the circus ground. The barbeque Craig had promised was already in full swing. Hunt could hear the sounds of merriment rising from between the assorted caravans long before he reached them. It was a joyful, almost musical sound which, unfortunately, lay at odds to Hunts' currently somber mood.

His sojourn by the sea had done little to lay to rest the dark thoughts coursing through his brain. There were still far too many unanswered questions for his liking. With some bitterness, he realized that the only way to get the answers he needed was for him to renew contact with the gruesome apparition of Andrew. This was not a pleasing proposition as he believed Andrew to be largely responsible for setting him on his current path in the first place.

Hunt stopped suddenly, his attention drawn to something as surprising as it was unwelcome. Over the past few weeks Hunt had grown accustomed to his altered vision. His
awareness of the life force energy flowing all around him was disturbing at first, but he found that, for the most part he was now able to tune it out, almost like a background noise. Daytime was easiest as natural daylight seemed to mute the visual impact of the energy waves he could see. During the night however, it was very different. Without the suns effect the world seemed to be permanently lit with a soft silvery sheen. Every person, beast, even every blade of grass seemed to glow with this inner light. All of this had become "normal" to Hunt over the past month, so much so that he barely gave it a second thought, until tonight.

As he stood at the edge of the circus ground Hunt noticed two things. The first was that an unfamiliar caravan had arrived during his absence. That, in itself, was not really remarkable. The circus workers came and went at all kinds of odd times, so a new caravan appearing was not really very alarming.

What had really caught his attention however was the light that came from this new caravan. There was a glow emanating from it as with all the others on the ground. This was not, however, the silvery, sparkling he had come to expect. The glow he now perceived was a deep, angry red. Whatever life force lay within that caravan was very different and far more dangerous than anything he had thus far encountered.

"Hey Joe!"

The voice tore hunts attention away from the caravan. It was Craig. He was approaching Hunt with a beer bottle in one hand and a huge grin on his face.

"Come on man! You're missing the party!" He took a swig
from the bottle. Judging by the slight wobble in his gait, Hunt guessed it wasn't his first that night. "I was starting to think you'd left us already." Craig said jovially as he reached Hunt, draping a friendly arm around his shoulder and guiding him towards the crowded barbeque pit.

As Hunt was led away, he cast a quick glance back towards the disturbing caravan. Just out of the corner of his eye, he could have sworn he saw the corner of a curtain flicker.

Any further thoughts of the caravan and its disturbing aura had to be put aside for the time being. With Craig's hand firmly at his back, Hunt found himself being thrust into the spotlight, rapidly becoming the center of attention at the barbeque. With burger in one hand and a bottle in the other, both provided by Sarah, Hunt virtually bounced from person to person as they all tried to engage him in conversation.

It was a strange experience for Hunt. While not entirely "one of them" the circus crowd had obviously accepted him into their very unique circle. Hunt suspected that Craig and Sarah had played a large part in this acceptance. They were well respected amongst the crew and performers alike and it seemed clear that their tacit approval of Hunt carried a lot of weight with everyone else.

Eventually, the atmosphere settled down into one of congenial banter and Hunt gradually found himself relaxing. Seating himself in one of the many fold-out camp chairs that were circled around the barbeque, he took the opportunity to observe the entertainment offered by his unexpected companions. These were people who worked hard and played even harder, they lived by their own rules and standards, caring little what the rest of the world thought of them. It was refreshing, almost liberating, to see such honesty.

As his gaze passed back and forth over the assembled throng, Hunt gradually became aware of a pair of eyes that were firmly fixed on him. With surprise he realized that he knew the owner of those eyes. He had encountered them earlier that same day, albeit from a distance. It was the young woman he had noticed watching him from her balcony during his journey to the beach. Here she was again, and again she was watching him. Hunt was unsure if he should feel flattered or disturbed by this.

"Having fun Joe?"

The question broke the moment. Hunt turned away from the woman to find Sarah, kneeling down next to his chair, a kind, gentle smile on her face. He smiled back.

"It's been a good night." He confirmed. Sarah smiled warmly.

"Well don't get used to it. It's back to the grind tomorrow so make sure you get some rest." She turned to leave but Hunt reached out, lightly taking her arm.

"Who's that woman Sarah?" He asked nodding his head in the direction of the young woman he had noticed earlier.

Sarah turned her head to look. The woman was no longer watching Hunt but was now engaged in conversation with one of the acrobats.

"She's one of the locals, a Circus groupie."

"A what?" Hunt asked.

"They're quite common really." Sarah explained. "People are fascinated with the Circus life. They like to be a part of it,
even if only for a short time. It's more common among the girls. They develop crushes on the more attractive artists."

As she was watching, Sarah noticed the young woman glance across at Hunt, when she saw Sarah watching her she dropped her gaze sheepishly. Sarah laughed softly.

"Not bad Joe." She said "One day on the show and you've got your first groupie, that's got to be some kind of record." She leaned in closer to Joe and whispered softly into his ear. "Just remember to save some energy for work tomorrow." Laughing easily, Sarah turned and walked away in the direction of her caravan.

Hunt's expression was one of bemusement as he watched Sarah's retreating back. It took him a little time to comprehend her meaning. When he did, he shook his head, smiling wryly at the thought. His smile faded rapidly however when he saw the young woman had started to cross the ground towards him.

The barbeque party was pretty much over now and the circus crowd was gradually filtering back to their respective caravans. Hunt watched the young woman glide across the grass, her movements full of grace and elegance. She knelt before him, her eyes never leaving his for an instant. Her delicate hand reached out.

"Hi, my name's Caroline. What's yours?"

Warily, Hunt took her hand, wishing above all else that, just for a moment, he could remove his gloves and feel the alabaster skin.

"Joe." He said somewhat gruffly.

"Nice to meet you Joe." She said sweetly. There was a
strange, almost sad lilt to her voice that Hunt found quite endearing. It spoke of a deep vulnerability and suddenly Hunt found himself wanting to get to know her better. "So what do you do here?" She asked.

"Not much really." Hunt admitted candidly. "I'm just passing through."

"I thought so" She nodded knowingly. "You don't look like you really belong here."

Hunt snorted derisively.

"I'm not sure where I belong anymore." He said softly.

They were silent for a time, lost in each other's thoughts and faces. Then Hunt noticed her shiver slightly. The night was drawing in and the temperature was dropping, she was still wearing the same bikini and sarong he had seen her in earlier that day.

"You're cold." He observed.

"It's late. I should really be getting home." She looked around them, noticing that the rest everyone had left now. They were alone. "Would you walk me? It's not far."

"Yes. Of course." Hunt responded without hesitation. He found himself strangely drawn to the petite, young woman. Helping her rise he realized, with some surprise, that his attraction was not really physical. She was an attractive woman, of that there was no doubt, but there was something more. An aura of pain, sadness and grief hung like a dark, brooding cloud over this woman. He could feel it and, alongside those feelings lay a deep vulnerability that made him want to protect her. But from what, he could not say.

She linked his arm and they walked towards the nearby
apartment blocks in silence. As they neared the edge of the circus ground Hunts' eye was once again drawn to the mysterious caravan he had noticed earlier that evening. It stood mute and alone, seemingly enshrouded within that same dark red aura that had so unnerved Hunt earlier. He couldn't explain why, but he felt a deep foreboding as he walked past. On some, almost instinctive level, Hunt knew that within the walls of that caravan lay danger, and possibly worse.

Caroline had felt him tense as they approached the caravan. She turned towards him, her face filled with concern.

"Is everything all right Joe?"

"Yes." Hunt answered firmly, putting the caravan out of his mind for the time being. "Everything is fine."

Hunt entered Caroline's apartment in a slightly bemused state of mind. He had surprised himself by accepting her invitation for a nightcap. Everything he was doing at the moment was so far out of character and totally at odds with his current situation, yet, for reasons he was at a loss to explain, it all felt right somehow, like it was supposed to be happening.

The apartment itself was a pleasant, if somewhat sparse two-bedroom affair. Its main feature was the extraordinary balcony that led off from the lounge area. As Hunt was guided around, he realized what it was that made the place feel so sterile. There were almost no personal effects on show. No ornaments, keepsakes and, as far as he could tell, no photos.

"Have you just moved in?" He asked innocently, completely unprepared for

Caroline's response. She visibly deflated shoulders and head dropping in obvious grief.

"Five years." She said softly in a voice close to breaking.

He looked around the living room in amazement. Five years, and still barely a sign of her presence. What had happened to her, he wondered.

Caroline saw the question forming on his face. She walked over to a cabinet set against the far wall. Fumbling for a few moments within one of the drawers, she finally found what she had been looking for. Walking back to Hunt in silence, she held a small black and white photo encased in a simple silver frame. He took it from her outstretched hand, noticing a slight tremor of nervousness as he did so.

It was a simple image, such as could be found in most households in the modern world. An image of carefree joy. Caroline and a handsome young man. They were smiling warmly, the mans' arms wrapped around her shoulders. It was a simple, elegant representation of a happier time.

"My husband." Caroline said simply by way of explanation. "He died four years ago."

"I'm sorry." Hunt said gently, sincerely. "I didn't mean to pry."

"It's ok, really." She assured him. "I don't know why, but I feel I can talk to you." As she looked at Hunt he could see the beginnings of a tear forming in her deep brown eyes. He wanted to reach out to her in that moment, reach out, enfold her in his arms and tell her that everything would be all right. He wanted to, but he didn't, he couldn't bring himself to offer a comfort he didn't truly believe.

"You don't have to talk about it." He said instead.

"I think I'd like to actually." She said. "If you don't mind listening?"

And so, talk she did. Taking seats at opposite ends of the plain, brown leather couch, Hunt listened attentively as Caroline proceeded to regale her tale of sorrow. It was faltering at first, she was unaccustomed to opening up in this manner but, with each sentence, her confidence gradually grew and the words became easier to find.

She told him of James, her husband of three years. How they had met at university and fallen immediately and hopelessly in love. Caroline spoke of the fun and laughter they had shared together until that fateful day when he had proposed and she had accepted. These were good memories, yet still laced with a patina of indescribable pain.

Their life together had started with such promise, so much so that it was easy for them to believe it would always be that way. That promise, however, began to evaporate the moment they moved to Eastbourne.

Under the premise of a new and exciting job opportunity for James, they had relocated, finding for themselves an exciting, newly appointed apartment block to begin this new stage in their adventure together. Unfortunately the job never really materialized. The company went bankrupt shortly after their move and James found himself joining the ever increasing line of young jobless. As the next year progressed, James worked tirelessly at a variety of dead-end, menial jobs in a vain effort to maintain their current standard of living. It was, ultimately, a losing battle. The financial pressures mounted steadily, drawing James deeper and deeper into a depressive state.

Caroline tried desperately to support her husband. She
maintained the home religiously, ensuring that, after a hard days' work, James always had somewhere peaceful to return to, with warm food on the table and an even warmer heart to enfold him. Her efforts served only to delay the inevitable. His depression marched inexorably onwards, dragging him ever on to depths where she could not follow.

Their last night together had been on the anniversary of their wedding. Three hard years they had been married and Caroline had wanted to do something special for him, something that would show him that all of the stress and worry and pain was worth it.

James had always had a love of the circus and there was one playing locally that night. As a surprise she had bought tickets for the evening performance. She just wanted them to have a night together where, even if only for a little while, they could put the stress of the world to one side and simply laugh and be happy. And, for a time they had. They had marveled at the acrobats, laughed at the clowns and been amazed by the magician. All the while, the cares of the real world seemed to have melted momentarily away. It was the happiest memory Caroline had of them together in the past year. Unfortunately it was also her last.

They had gone to sleep that night entwined in each other's loving embrace. When morning came, Caroline found she was alone. At some point during the night James had left.

Two days later his car had been found, abandoned on a remote car park at Beachy Head. His body was discovered a short time later, tangled in the rocks at the base of the cliffs. Suicide was the official conclusion. Tomorrow marked the four year anniversary of his death.

Hunt had listened to all of this with a growing sadness. As she had talked the two of them had drawn ever closer together on the couch until now, at the culmination of her desperate tale, Caroline found herself crying into his chest, his strong arms encircling her comfortingly. He held her close, his gloved hand stroking her hair soothingly.

After a time her weeping subsided, then stopped and Hunt realized that her grief had exhausted her so completely that she had fallen asleep in his arms. Carefully he rose from the couch, scooping her tenderly into his arms and carrying her through to the bedroom. Laying her gently upon the bed he covered her with the soft down-filled duvet, stroking the hair away from her face. As he rose to leave her hand suddenly reached out, grabbing him by the wrist.

"Please, don't go." She murmured softly, not quite awake. He eased her hand gently back under the covers and knelt at her face.

"Don't worry, I'll be here when you wake up." He whispered.

Moving to the opposite side of the bed Hunt lay on top of the duvet. Rolling onto his side and laying an arm across her waist which she quickly grabbed, pulling him closer towards her.

"Sleep now." Hunt whispered softly. "I'll keep you safe."

"Thank you." Came the gentle murmur as Caroline finally, completely succumbed to the night.

Chapter 12

Hunt drew some amused glances as he returned to the circus ground just after ten o'clock the next morning. Craig was sitting outside his caravan with a mug of steaming tea. He waved Hunt over, a wry smile on his face.

"I take it you found a better alternative to the wagon last night then?" He asked slyly. Hunt had the decency to blush. Before he could respond however, Sarah poked her head out of the caravan door.

"Morning Joe." She said brightly. "I'm just dishing breakfast up. Want some?"

The enticing smells of fresh cooked bacon and sausages appealed directly to Hunts' stomach.

"That would be wonderful. Thank you." He said without hesitation. Sarah disappeared and Hunt turned his attention back to Craig who continued to eye him with a knowing smile.

"Nothing happened." Hunt declared.

"If you say so, Joe." Craig said, though it was clear from his tone that he didn't believe a word of it. "I have to say though, your reputation with the boys has gone through the roof after last night."

"I'll bet."

Craig stood and led the way back into the caravan with Hunt following close behind.

"I'd keep out of the way of the acrobats though." Craig continued with some amusement as he took a seat at the table.

"Oh?" Hunt queried.

"Yes, you're definitely not in their good books right now." Sarah laughed. "They'd been eying that girl up all night then you stroll in and poof….., they may as well have not existed."

"Oh God, yes." Craig chuckled. "The best of it was that you never said a word to her. You've got some talent there pal. Maybe I should get you to teach me a few things eh?" He gave a sly wink.

"You watch yourself my lad!" Sarah warned with mock severity.

Hunt couldn't help but smile at the playful banter between the two of them. It was easy to relax in their company and he was thankful for that.

Breakfast was a relaxed, pleasant affair. Craig and Sarah continued their joking throughout and didn't seem to mind Hunts silence. For his part the time allowed him to think on the events of the previous evening.

Caroline seemed much improved when he had left her that morning. She had effectively purged herself of a range of negative emotions which had been allowed to build up over the previous years and now, at last, the healing process could truly start. Today was the anniversary of her husbands' death and, in memory of that event she intended to come to the evening performance. Perhaps she felt that she could, in some way, relive those last memories of joy and peace. Hunt wasn't convinced but, that didn't matter. He couldn't deny that he was looking forward to seeing her again.

Then it was time for the working day to begin. They had two shows to perform that day and, so far, Hunt had no idea what was expected of him.

Chapter 13

D.I. Cunningham had had an easy, if tedious start to the day. If there was one thing he hated, it was paperwork, but then, he knew of no officer that truly loved all the form-filling and filing that, even in this so-called "computer-age", seemed to dominate their profession. Still, his sense of order and professionalism required that he knuckle down and set his mind to the task at hand. Currently that entailed the completion of his report regarding the unusual murders earlier that week.

To say that this case still bothered him was a gross understatement, it irritated him beyond measure. Everything about this case was wrong in a way he couldn't quite put his finger on, from the unusual nature of the deaths of the two young boys to the sudden and dramatic involvement of MI5.

Now, after thirty minutes of staring at a blank form he felt like tossing the whole thing across the room in disgust. He probably would have as well, were it not for the sudden, discreet knock at his door. Taking a deep breath he looked up
to see the round face of one of the uniformed Sergeants looking in at him through the single pane of glass in the door. Cunningham waved for the man to come in.

"Sorry to disturb you sir." The man said politely as he entered, closing the door softly behind him. "Only this is something I thought you'd want to see." He indicated a slim file he was carrying under one arm.

"That's quite all right Sergeant." Cunningham assured the man. I'm glad of the distraction. What have you got for me?"

"You were working that murder case weren't you Sir? The one that got taken over by MI5?"

Cunningham's eyes narrowed suspiciously for a moment.

"Why do you think I'm in such a good mood?"

"Things not going well then?" Cunningham was not sure if the man was playing dumb or if he was totally immune to sarcasm. It was only the look of total honesty on the Sergeants face that convinced him that this was not a prank.

"I've been staring at this form for longer than I care to think about." Cunningham said, angrily wafting the offending piece of paper in front of the bemused Sergeants face. "And there is not a single thing I can write on it. Cause of death? How the hell do I know what the cause of death was. Bloody MI5 took both bodies away yesterday along with every scrap of evidence related to the case. Every photo, report, memo, damn it, they even took my god damned note book. So you tell me Sergeant. How do you think it's going?"

The Sergeant had been steadily backing away during Cunningham's tirade. The look on the poor mans' face almost made the angry D.I. laugh out loud. If nothing else, it certainly served to douse his anger. Cunningham shook his head ruefully.

"I'm sorry Sergeant. I didn't mean to have a go at you. This has just got me so wound up at the moment."

"Maybe this will help then sir." The Sergeant offered calmly placing a thumb drive on the desk. Cunningham looked from the drive back to the Sergeant.

"Do you want to explain what this is?"

"In the early hours of this morning Sir, I was called out to a fire out on one of the old industrial estates. The fire brigade was on the scene by the time I arrived. It was a burned out car Sir."

"Probably some kids out joy-riding." Cunningham surmised. "What of it?"

"I thought the same at first, to be honest. But it was a very expensive Merc. that had been trashed and I thought it odd that a car of that value hadn't been reported stolen. Anyway, we ran the plates and, you'll never guess who came back as the owner."

The Sergeant laid the file on Cunningham's desk, opening it to the single sheet of paper it contained. The breath immediately caught in Cunningham's throat.

"You double-checked this?" Cunningham asked, his eyes never leaving the paper before him.

"Absolutely Sir."

The paper contained a copy of the driving license that would have belonged to the vehicles owner. Cunningham didn't need to read the name on it. The picture was enough. There was no way he could mistake a face as strikingly beautiful as hers. Jane D'Arcy. Agent Jane D'Arcy of MI5.

"Was there any sign of her?" Cunningham asked.

"No Sir. We've got SOCO going over the vehicle now but initial findings indicate that she wasn't in the vehicle when the fire was set. We did, however, find her phone."

"And?"

"Well, it was pretty trashed. It was on the passenger seat, so the fire hit it pretty hard. I've had the tech guys going over it all morning. So far all they've managed to recover is a voice mail that had been left for her yesterday."

"Is this it?" Cunningham asked, indicating the thumb drive.

"Yes Sir. I figured you might want to listen to it yourself."

Cunningham was intrigued. He took the drive and inserted it into a vacant u.s.b. port on his computer. It took a moment for his system to identify the drive before providing him with the option of viewing the files. There was only the one file, a simple media file which Cunningham immediately clicked on.

For several moments the only sound in the room was the disembodied voice of Mantle as his last message to Jane was replayed.

"That bitch." Cunningham exclaimed softly once the message had ended. "She knew he was alive all along." He looked across at the Sergeant. "Do we know if she got this message?"

"According to the techs, that message hadn't been played back Sir."

Cunningham removed the thumb drive and laid it on the desk in front of him.

"Who else knows about this?" Cunningham asked eventually.

"Aside from us, just the tech Sir."

"Let's keep it that way for the moment shall we."

"You're not giving this to MI5 then?" The Sergeant queried cautiously. "It is their case after all."

"I'm afraid I have to correct you there. Their case was the murder of two young teenage boys. The case I intend to investigate is one of arson, and, until I say otherwise, those two cases are not connected. Do I make myself clear?"

"Absolutely, Sir." The Sergeant smiled knowingly.

"Thank you for bringing this to my attention Sergeant. Now, if you don't mind, I have some work to get back to."

"Of course, Sir."

Cunningham watched the Sergeant leave the room, once more closing the door behind him. All the while, the D.I.'s mind was racing. He knew he was taking a big risk here. If the Superintendent got wind of what he was doing he could well end up back in uniform before the end of the week. That didn't matter. Cunningham had to know what was going on. Instinctively he knew this was something more than a case of domestic terrorism.

"I think it's time we had a conversation, Mr. Mantle." Cunningham said softly to himself.

Knowing this would either make or break his career, Cunningham rose and headed towards the door, pocketing the thumb drive and grabbing his coat on the way.

Chapter 14

For the first hour or so, Hunt felt lost. Everyone on the show seemed to have their own clearly defined role to play in order to prepare for the coming performances, so he was left largely to his own devices.

He wandered around the tent, watching in fascination as people scurried back and forth. There was a quiet intensity and excitement that seemed to build with each passing moment. Concession stands appeared just inside the entrance of the tent while artists ran back and forth from the rear exit, bringing props and costumes into the back stage area and arranging them just so. The sound and lighting technicians performed last minute checks on all the equipment.

Hunt was actually glad of the time alone. He was still bothered by the implications of the new arrival he had observed the previous evening. Seen in daylight the caravan was nowhere near as sinister in appearance as it had first seemed. The muting effect of the morning sun made the disturbing red glow appear little more than a murky haze. But it was still there.

A few discreet questions to Craig and Sarah earlier that day had revealed the occupants to be a father and son partnership. They were the show Clowns and claimed to be descended from the Grimaldi family but Craig had doubts about that. It seemed that no-one really knew a lot about them, they didn't associate with the rest of the troupe, preferring to keep themselves to themselves.

No-one was really paying Hunt much attention at the moment, so focused were they on their pre-performance preparations. This gave him the perfect opportunity to discreetly observe the Father-Son clown team as they went about their own tasks.

Hunt quickly realized that, were it not for his altered sight, he would have found the two men utterly unremarkable. The father was a relatively tall, balding man. It was obvious that, in his youth, he had been a powerful man but advancing years had turned much of his former bulk to flab. He filled his clown suit to capacity now, but still retained a surprising degree of agility and dexterity. His son, meanwhile, was a good head shorter than his father. Currently he had discarded his clown jacket and was wearing a tight fitting red and white striped shirt which showed off an impressive upper body. Of all the acts theirs was the one which required the most varied number of props and paraphernalia. It took the two of them quite some time to arrange the tools of their trade exactly to their liking.

The only oddity that his normal vision reported to Hunt
was the demeanor of both men. The son was a veritable dynamo of energy, bustling to and fro from caravan to tent at a pace that was exhausting to watch. Yet both of them maintained a uniformly sour expression. On other artists this would not have been all that surprising but Hunt would have expected those

with clowning as a profession to display far more natural good humor. They barely uttered a word to any of their colleagues; in fact, it seemed to Hunt that the rest of the troupe actively tried to avoid any interaction.

But Hunt saw more than ordinary people, and what he observed now he found to be intensely curious. The Father seemed to carry with him the same aura that Hunt had detected around the caravan. While that was itself interesting, what really captured Hunts' attention was the fact that the older clown was not the source of the aura. Even in daylight Hunt could see that the aura surrounding the father was not as intense as that which surrounded the caravan. Even more interesting however, was the clearly defined pulsing line which seemed to connect the man to his abode. It looked, for all the world, as if he was permanently tethered to whatever lay within the caravan. This was a new phenomenon for Hunt, and he didn't quite know what to make of it.

"Joe!"

Sarah's cheerful call effectively cut through Hunts' thoughts. He turned to see her beaming face approaching him.

"I've been looking all over for you Joe. We have work to do."

Hunt smiled as she took him by the arm and began leading him off towards the main entrance of the tent. She was babbling merrily away to him all the while.

It seemed that Hunt was expected to be on door duty to start with. This involved making sure all of the audience members had valid tickets for the show. As there was no such thing as numbered seating he, thankfully, did not have to guide anyone to specific seating areas, so the level of communication with the general public was blessedly small. His only other task was litter duty. As this took place only during the interval and at the end of the performance he would get an opportunity to see the show itself.

Hunt found himself reacting to the general buzz that was building amongst his co-workers. It shouldn't have been all that surprising really as it was the first time he had ever witnessed a real, live circus. Somehow it managed to bring out a little of whatever child remained within him. He smiled despite himself.

It wasn't long before the audience began to arrive. Some arrived by car, leaving their vehicles in the parking area that lay at the edge of the park. But most walked, heading towards the circus from all directions. The majority of the audience consisted of families with children ranging in age from four to fourteen. There were some couples and even a few pensioners, but these were definitely in a minority. The background hum of excited conversation began to rise as the tent gradually filled to capacity.

Hunt had been steadily taking tickets off the customers as they entered, tearing off the stubs and returning them to their
owners when suddenly he stopped. Hunt hadn't really been taking the time to observe the customers, maintaining his focus on the tickets only. This customer, however, was different from the rest.

There weren't many people who would think of turning up to a circus dressed in a well-tailored suit, nor would they walk across a grassy field in highly polished, expensive, patent leather shoes. As Hunt returned the ticket to the man in question he felt an almost physical shock of recognition. Fear and surprise rose in equal measure within him as he stared into the face of a man he had not seen in several weeks and certainly never expected to see now, especially not in a place like this. It was his former doctor, one of the key figures responsible for his recovery following his accident so many months ago.

For his part Mantle derived no small amount of amusement at the bemused expression on the face of his former patient, though he was very careful not to let it show. Maintaining a cool detachment, the former doctor, turned MI5 agent calmly took the offered ticket stub and carried on into the tent to locate a good vantage point from which he could view the proceedings.

Hunt watched the doctor walk casually away. He was not a man who believed in coincidences and, even if he were, this would have been too large a coincidence to ignore. His suspicions aroused, Hunt had to fight to keep his face from scowling. Sarah noticed the change in his demeanor all the same. As the last of the customers passed them by, she moved closer to him.

"Are you ok?" She asked, her voice mirroring the concern on her face.

"I'm fine." Hunt tried a reassuring smile with only minimal success. "Just tired I guess. So what's next?"

"Take a pew." She indicated an empty seat in the front row of the right side seating bank. "Enjoy the show. I'll come and get you when it's time for the clean-up."

Mantle watched surreptitiously from his position midway up the center seating block as Hunt took a seat at ringside. Initially he had been surprised that Hunt had settled with such apparent ease in this environment. He appeared to have been completely accepted. Upon further consideration however, Mantle realized that the Circus was perfectly suited to Hunts' needs at the moment. They didn't tend to ask a lot of questions so long as you kept your head down and did your job and, as far as the authorities were concerned, they were practically invisible. Moving as frequently and erratically as they generally did made them the ideal place to be if you wanted to stay off the radar. Despite the many frustrations of the past few weeks, Mantle was forced to admit that he was more than a little impressed with the resourcefulness of his former patient. It was becoming clear now that he, along with many others he suspected, had seriously underestimated the man.

Chapter 15

Mantle found the performance more than a little tedious. It wasn't the first time he had seen a circus and, compared to those he had viewed in the past, this one was very basic, to say the least. Still, the children seemed to be enjoying themselves.

In truth, Mantle spent more time observing Hunt than he did the activities in the ring. There was an air of tenseness about the man which had set alarm bells off in the MI5 Agents' brain. He knew his appearance had shaken Hunt, but he instinctively felt there was more to it than that.

It was when the clowns first appeared that Mantle knew there was something not quite right. While the former doctor did not have the benefit of Hunts' unusual visual gifts he had, nevertheless, been a part of this strange new world, to which his patient had only recently become a member, for quite some time. His instincts had developed a fine edge over the years. Even without the visual prompt of Hunts' increased tension, Mantle would have known something was amiss. He couldn't quite put his finger on it, but something definitely felt wrong.

For Hunts' part, the appearance of the clowns had indeed heightened his anxiety. The hazy red glow persisted around the elder clown, the pulsating line of dark energy tracing its way back out of the rear exit, leading the way, Hunt knew, back to their caravan and whatever disturbing entity it contained.

The clowns pranced, danced and fooled around, entertaining the audience with their antics, blithely unaware of the intense scrutiny they were under from two specific individuals. Both Hunt and Mantle knew something was disturbingly wrong, equally both men had no idea exactly what that thing was.

Raucous applause and ear splitting cheering signaled the end of the show. The audience began to file out of the tent amidst the laughter and excited chatter of happy children being led by contented parents. Hunt was grateful to see that Mantle joined the mass. He had half-expected a confrontation with the man and that was something he was not prepared for.

The after-show cleanup progressed quickly. As he looked at the rapidly accumulating bags of rubbish, Hunt found himself amazed at just how much could be generated by so few in such a short space of time. They filled five heavy duty refuse sacks in total. It would be someone's job at the end of the day to transport these to the nearest recycling center, but that wasn't Hunts' problem.

He placed the last of the rubbish piles on the ground outside the rear entrance to the tent, as he did so Sarah approached him wearing her now familiar smile.

"That wasn't too bad." She said brightly. "One more show and we're done for the day."

"What time is the next show?" Hunt asked.

"The performance starts at seven, so we've got a few hours now. I'm going to put some food on in a few minutes. You're welcome to join us if you fancy."

Hunt barely heard her. Glancing over Sarah's shoulder, he could see across the field to the car park. A number of the circus patrons had made use of this and, as he watched, the place was steadily emptying. One car in particular drew his attention however. Small, sleek and olive green in color, it's owner standing with his back against the side panel, arms folded across his chest. Even at this distance Hunt could feel the laser-beam gaze was directed at himself. It was Mantle.

"Joe?"

Hunt tore his gaze away from his former physician, his brain rapidly trying to recall Sarah's last words to him.

"You're really not with it today, are you?" Sarah observed.

"Sorry. Long night. What was it you asked?"

"I wanted to know if you'd be joining us for tea tonight?"

"Oh, right." Hunt paused, his gaze returning to the car park and the persistent Doctor Mantle. "You know, I think I'll pass on that if you don't mind?" He said eventually. "I feel like taking a walk actually." He began moving away before Sarah had a chance to voice an objection.

Still walking, he turned back to a slightly bemused Sarah. "Seven o'clock you said?" With a shrug she nodded. "I'll be back before then." With a slight wave he turned away.

Mantle watched Hunts' approach. It was clear from his gait and general carriage that his former patient was not a happy man. Not surprising really, Mantle sympathized, considering everything that had happened to him over the course of the past month.

"You're a long way from home." The bluntness of Hunt's greeting spoke volumes as to the degree of his displeasure. Mantle brushed it aside easily.

"It's good to see you too John." He smiled wryly.

Hunt came to a stop directly in front of his former doctor. The two men eyed each other in silence, Hunt taking careful note of the well-tailored suit and expensive vehicle.

"What are you doing here?" Hunt asked eventually.

"Would you believe me if I said I was checking up on my patient?"

"Not for a second."

"No, I suppose you wouldn't" Mantle conceded, the wry smile never leaving his face. "Are you hungry John?"

"Pardon?" Mantles' easy-going attitude was starting to get to Hunt.

"You have questions. I have answers, some of them at least. Why don't we put those things together over a spot of lunch?"

Even Hunt had to concede that it was a reasonable suggestion. It had been some time since breakfast and, in truth, he was quite hungry. Mantle could see Hunt begin to relax a little.

"Come on John." Opening the drivers' side door and waving John to the opposite side. "Get in, please."

They drove in silence, the journey itself proving to be surprisingly short. Mantle noted the quizzical look Hunt aimed in his direction as he smoothly pulled into a parking space outside a twenty-four hour McDonalds located only a short distance from the circus ground.

"What can I say?" He said in response to the unspoken question. "It's a weakness of mine, a guilty pleasure if you like."

They had arrived during that period of the day which was traditionally quiet in such places, being too late for the lunchtime crowd and too early for the night time revelers seeking their post alcohol sustenance.

Taking a window table which afforded a view of the parking lot the two men removed the wrapping from their burgers and began to eat. Mantle felt it was important for Hunt to decide how he wanted the conversation to begin, so he ate steadily, content simply to observe his lunch companion in silence.

"How did you find me?" Hunt asked eventually between mouthfuls.

"That's not really the question you want to ask, is it John?"

It was a surprisingly astute observation, but one which Hunt quickly dismissed.

"Perhaps not. But it's as good a place as any for us to start."

"Fair enough." Mantle conceded amiably. "In truth John, you've done very well, far better than I expected in fact. Had it not been for this past week, well….you simply made too much noise."

"It wasn't my fault." Hunt said softly. "They attacked me." His mind jumped back to the attempted mugging. The fight. The blow to the head. The intense need. He could see the expressions on the boys faces as he drew the life force out of them, fed off them. Suddenly Hunt tossed the remnants of his burger on the table in disgust, his appetite had gone completely. Now, he just felt nauseated and angry.

"You lied to me." He accused suddenly. Mantle looked momentarily confused. "When I last saw you, I asked you if I had changed in any way. You said no. That was a lie."

"You are mistaken John. I did not lie. I may have been a little… conservative with the truth."

"What the hell is that supposed to mean?" Hunt spat vehemently.

"You asked me if you had changed. If death had changed you. I told you it hadn't. That was true."

"What do you call this then?"

"You did not gain these new abilities as a result of your death John. They've always been there, hidden in some unused corner of your mind. Your death simply gave you an opportunity to access them." He could see the disbelief and confusion in Hunts' face. It was hard not to feel sympathy for the man. Mantle sighed heavily. "Let me try and explain John." Mantle continued softly. "All of your life, this power, ability, whatever you want to call it. It's been there, lurking away in your brain, but there's been a wall between you and it, a wall you never even knew existed. And you never knew because you never needed to know. You were never in a situation where that knowledge would be of any use or benefit to you, until you died. Then the wall came down and, for the first time, you were forced, not only to acknowledge the presence of this power, but also to reach out, to grab it in both hands and to use it. From that point there was no going back. You stopped being John Hunt, the arrogant reporter who cared about nothing and no-one and became...."

"A murderer." Hunt stated flatly.

"If that's what you choose to be."

"I don't have a choice! You've seen what I can do!"

It was clear that Hunt was firmly mired in a bog of self-recrimination and loathing. Mantle knew it would take something fairly substantial to break him free.

A young family chose that moment to walk in. Mantle watched as the two parents walked either side of their young girl, he guessed her age to be around four or five. The parents each held one of the girls' hands and she hopped and bounced excitedly between them, babbling away merrily as young children are wont to do. It was a very normal and pleasing sight and the more he watched it, the more an idea formed in Mantle's mind. He turned back to Hunt.

"Let me ask you a question John." He began slowly. "If you were to take that young girl by the hand, what would stop you from crushing her fingers or ripping her arm out of its socket?"

"What kind of question is that?" Hunt demanded incredulously.

"Wait a minute John." Mantle held up a hand in a soothing gesture. "I'm not talking about the ethical or moral aspects of the situation. Think about it for a moment. You are fairly strong, above average for a man of your age and build I'd guess. Pound for pound you outstrip that child by a considerably margin. So,

I ask again, on a purely physical level, what is it that stops you from harming such a child?"

"You're talking about control, aren't you?"

"Exactly!" Mantle exclaimed. "From the moment you were born you have been blessed with the physical gift of strength. But, you've had to learn to control it, and you've spent all your life learning how to do that haven't you?"

"I guess so." Hunt responded dubiously. It was clear that he had not made the connection Mantle had been hoping for.

"Ok then, so tell me John, what do you think would happen if you were given that gift of strength say,…six weeks ago? Do you think you could still go up and shake that girl by the hand, or pick her up in an embrace without inadvertently causing some kind of damage?"

Mantle began to see a glimmer of realization dawning on Hunts' face. There were still doubts, however.

"Ok, I get where you're going with this." Hunt conceded finally, much to Mantles' relief. "But, as a child I had people to teach me. I had parents and society, school,…" He looked up suddenly, a wry smile on his face. "If you tell me now that Hogwarts is real, I'm going to get up and leave, you know that don't you?"

Mantle laughed. If Hunt could find humor in all this then, perhaps there was still hope.

"No John, I promise. No Hogwarts."

"Thank God." Hunt breathed earnestly. "But you do get my point don't you?"

"I do indeed." Mantle assured him.

"So, how can I learn if there's no-one to teach me?"

"What makes you think there is no-one to teach you John?"

Hunt paused for a moment, studying the open, honest face of his former doctor. Finally, realization dawned in full.

"You?"

Mantle smiled broadly.

"I swear though, if you ever call me Dad, we will have a problem."

They both laughed then. For the first time since he had woken up in the hospital so many weeks ago, Hunt actually began to feel hopeful. He had come to believe himself to be a monster, forced to kill indiscriminately in order to maintain his existence. Now, for the first time, he began to see the possibility for him to be something else. He still didn't know what that something was, but he wanted to believe that it could be something better.

Once the laughter had died down Hunt grew serious once more. There were still plenty of questions to which he needed answers.

"You're not really a doctor are you?" He asked. Mantle shook his head, smiling still.

"Although I do hold all of the necessary qualifications."

"So, what then?" Hunt pressed. Mantle reached into his inside jacket pocket, withdrawing a small, black leather wallet which he opened and lay on the table. Hunt picked it up, examining the Identification Card closely.

"MI5?" Hunts' eyebrows raised in surprise. "Should I be impressed, or worried?"

"Neither." Mantle assured him. "It's a convenient fiction which allowed us access to a number of valuable resources."

"Us?" Hunt pounced on the word.

"You didn't think I worked alone did you?"

"To be honest, I hadn't really thought about it at all." Hunt admitted candidly. "Who else is there then?"

"You've already met my partner."

Hunts' eyebrows furrowed in momentary confusion as his mind searched back over the memories of the past few weeks. He clicked his fingers suddenly, a triumphant expression on his face.

"Jane!" He exclaimed. This was the nurse who had been by his side throughout his recovery and then mysteriously re-appeared in such dramatic fashion, saving him from the thugs in the alley. How could he have forgotten her? "So where is she then?"

"Cleaning up your mess back in Bath." Mantle answered seriously. "She should join us soon."

"So what happens next?"

"That's largely up to you John. But, if you want my advice, I think it's time we were moving on."

"That's not going to happen just yet." Hunt said cautiously. Mantle frowned.

"What's the problem?"

In as succinct a manner as he could manage, Hunt carefully detailed his misgivings regarding the circus and, more specifically, the clowns. Mantle listened intently, a thoughtful expression on his face. When he had finished Hunt examined his new mentors face intently, hoping to get some clue as to what the man might be thinking.

"Interesting." Was Mantles' only response.

"You don't believe me, do you?" Hunt asked, the disappointment evident in his tone. Mantle shook his head.

"Quite the contrary John." Mantle assured him quickly. "I'm not going to doubt the veracity of your sight, or your instincts. I would be a fool to do so. I'm just considering the best course of action from this point forward."

Hunt was visibly relieved. So much so in fact, that it gave him the confidence to offer his own suggestion.

"The show has another performance tonight. I'm going back there. Maybe I can find out something more useful."

"In the mean-time, perhaps I can use my MI5 resources and run a few discreet checks on both the circus and this father and son clown team."

"I'd appreciate that."

"I'm here to help, John. How about I meet you on the car park tomorrow morning and we can compare notes?"

"That sounds like a good plan, Doc." Hunt said with a slight smile.

Mantle was surprised at the sudden use of his old title.

"I'm not your doctor any more you know"

"I know." Hunt admitted. "But that's what you were to me when I first knew you. At the time I trusted you, I respected your opinion, your advice. Somehow, it helps to still think of you that way. Does it bother you?"

"Well it's a fact, I've been called worse in my life." Mantle smiled a little sardonically. "No John, it doesn't bother me."

"Are you going to give me a lift back to the show then?"

"A word of caution first." Mantle said seriously. "You are only now beginning to understand the nature of your powers. Please do us both a favor and don't launch headlong into anything stupid. It would be a real shame if anything happened to you now we are just starting to get to know each other."

"Don't worry. Until I have a better understanding of all of this, I have no intention of doing anything more than is absolutely necessary. I'll be careful."

Chapter 16

By the time Mantle pulled back onto the car park neighboring the circus ground, Hunt was feeling better than he had done in some time. It was only now that he realized just how lost and isolated he had begun to feel. While the problems themselves had not magically evaporated during the course of their conversation, the devastating effect they had had upon his psyche had diminished noticeably. Hunt was no longer alone. If nothing else, at the very least he had someone to talk to who, if they did not completely understand, would at least not think him mad. It was surprising just what a difference that made.

Exiting the sleek Jaguar, he felt energized for the first time since leaving the Exodus all those weeks ago. His step was lighter as he crossed the grassy field towards the tent, walking with a confidence that had been absent for what seemed an age. Until now he had believed this new found ability to be nothing more than a curse and worse, something that operated totally outside his conscious control, a pure survival instinct. Since talking with Mantle, Hunt found himself reevaluating his situation, especially the extraordinary things he could now do. If he could exert control, what were the possibilities?

So engrossed was he in his own thoughts that Hunt did not immediately notice the images his altered vision were sending him. It had been his intent to rest and think alone for a time, there still being over an hour until preparations would begin for the evening show. The only place where he thought he could rest undisturbed would be in the tent itself and that was exactly where he was now headed. His first warning that something was amiss was the raised voices carried on the sun-heated afternoon air. They originated from within the tent, more specifically, the backstage area which Hunt was now approaching. He paused, moving to the side of the performers' entrance as he finally noticed what had been evident all along, the ethereal, pulsing red trail that snaked back to the clowns' caravan, the old clowns' tether.

"We can't keep doing this!" The voice was strong, but there was a note of pleading to it.

"We don't have a choice." This second voice, tired, worn with age and an undefinable sadness.

The old clown and his son Hunt surmised. Easing himself quietly towards the opening, he strained to listen.

"But we're killing people!" The younger voice declared desperately.

"You don't know that!"

"I can read Dad! It's in the papers if you know where to look for it."

"Coincidence." The older clown said dismissively.

"Come on Dad. You don't believe that any more than I do."

"It doesn't matter what I believe. We don't have a choice!"

"There has to be a way to stop it." The son pleaded with his father.

"I tried that, remember? Seven years ago? I tried to stop it, and look what happened."

"Mums death wasn't your fault Dad." The younger man said softly, voice tinged with sadness and loss.

"Look son, we have always been the keeper of this secret, this curse, and we always will be. We can't fight it, we can't change it. I fought with my father over this the same way you're fighting with me. It made no difference then and it makes no difference now. This is who we are. This is what we do."

"So you're going to do what it wants tonight? You're going to sign someone else's death warrant?"

"Rather them than us."

The conversation appeared to have reached a natural conclusion. Hunt moved quietly away from the tent before either of the clowns exited. He had heard more than enough now to confirm his earlier suspicions; unfortunately it still wasn't enough to tell him exactly what was going on. Whatever it was, it was going to happen tonight and that posed a problem for Hunt.

In Mantle, Hunt had found a new ally, one he could really use right now. Unfortunately it would be morning before they met again and, during all of their conversations Hunt had never once thought of getting Mantles' contact details. This meant that, despite everything positive that had happened that day, now, when it really mattered, Hunt still found himself to be alone.

159 | Fool In The Ring

Chapter 17

Showtime approached faster than Hunt would have liked. He had replayed the overheard conversation in his mind time and again, looking for anything that might give him some idea of what to expect. It was all in vain and now he found himself once more standing at the main entrance to the tent taking tickets from unsuspecting and joyous customers, all the while dreading what the night may bring.

Not a single face registered with Hunt as the seemingly endless stream of customers flowed passed him. Tickets were taken and stubs returned in a robotic fashion, devoid of thought. With a barely concealed air of desperation Hunt found himself searching the tent, eyes scanning constantly, hoping against hope that he would gain some insight, some clue as to what he may be facing that night.

A soft, delicate touch on his hand forced his attention back to the current task. Looking down, Hunt was momentarily surprised to see Caroline, her deep brown eyes boring into him. He had forgotten that she was attending the evenings' performance.

"Are you okay Joe?" She asked softly.

Hunt wanted to tell her. He knew he should warn her. Convince her to get away from this place. But he couldn't. There was nothing he could say that would make any sense.

"I'm fine." Was all he could manage.to say in the end. She smiled sweetly, a hint of nervousness making the edges of her mouth twitch slightly.

"Will I see you after the show?" She asked.

"Sure." Hunt promised. "I'll come and find you after we've cleaned up."

"I'll wait for you then." She said relief evident in her tone.

Hunt watched her head deeper into the tent. The attentions of the remaining customers forced him to turn away for a moment and when he turned back to try to find her, she was gone.

With mounting anxiety, Hunt continued processing tickets until, finally, the line had cleared. All the seats were full this evening so he was forced to stand between the two seating banks that formed the entry way. Moving as far forward as he could without interfering with the view for the paying customers, Hunt began searching the audience, looking for Caroline.

He found her with relative ease, seated in the front row of the center aisle. He guessed she had chosen a similar position to the one she had occupied with her late husband on that fateful night four years previously. Hunt was undecided as to whether her position was beneficial or not under the current

circumstances. At least he could find and reach her quickly should anything untoward happened. Unfortunately this also meant that she made a very easy target. Despite the fact that Hunt had only known the woman for barely a day, he felt strangely connected to her. He was determined to protect her if at all possible.

The house lights begin to dim. Hunt felt his muscles tense involuntarily. The show was about to start. In truth, he did not expect anything to happen at the moment. All of his information so far pointed towards the father and son clown team as being the instigators of whatever was to come. There was no indication whatsoever that the rest of the circus was involved in any way. Still, he remained alert and ready to act nevertheless. This was not the time for complacency.

There was little to differentiate this show from the one he had witnessed earlier that same day. The artists performed their individual segments with practiced ease, thrilling and exciting the audience with every move. Despite himself, Hunt allowed his body to relax a little. The longer the show progressed without incident, the more Hunt believed he may have been mistaken, that he had somehow misinterpreted the meaning of the overheard conversation.

It was not until the second half that the clowns made their appearance. Despite his personal misgivings, the only thunderclap, or explosion they heralded was one of laughter and applause. It was well-earned. The two men worked in concert, providing the audience with a slick, well presented routine full of spills and gags of every kind. So slick were they in fact, that it took Hunt several moments to realize that the performance had changed slightly from the one they had delivered earlier that day.

It was only a minor alteration which was why it had taken Hunt so long to become aware of it. The first show had both men very much centered in the ring itself. They would occasionally approach the ringside but there was very little direct interaction with the audience. That was not the case with this performance.

The son still maintained his position within the ring while his father took himself onto the seating stands themselves. Amidst cries of delight the old clown danced and pranced amongst the audience with a surprising amount of energy. Hunt studied the man carefully as he bounced erratically from one laughing customer to the next. As strange as it seemed, Hunt was sure the man was searching for something. Hunts brow furrowed in concentration as he observed the strange proceedings. From customer to customer the clown bounced until almost inevitably his unpredictable cavorting brought him before Caroline.

No matter how many times Hunt replayed the events in his mind he would never be entirely sure what he had witnessed. There appeared to be a sudden, albeit slight change in the clowns' demeanor as he approached Caroline. Then, without warning, he tripped on his wildly over-sized shoes, falling headlong into her lap. The audience laughed uproariously while Caroline blushed furiously, openly embarrassed at being thrust into the spotlight in this manner. The old clown picked himself up, swaying in an obviously theatrical manner. He dusted himself off with a massive
handkerchief which conveniently concealed a wealth of sparkling confetti meant to imitate dust, all of which covered the immediate audience. Leaning forward, he then planted a make-up laden kiss on Caroline's cheek and danced back into the ring.

This signaled the end of the performance. The clowns left amidst riotous applause, the next act appeared and the show continued without missing a beat. Everything was as it should be and, for Hunt, that was perhaps most disturbing of all.

He knew without question that something unusual had happened, yet he had absolutely no idea what it was. As much as he began to relax following the clowns' departure, at the same time he felt a seething frustration brewing. Despite his foreknowledge of their intent, Hunt had proven totally powerless to stop them. Worse still, he had absolutely no idea what they had even done. Not for the first time, he felt himself to be totally out of his depth in this strange new world he had been unwillingly thrust into.

Since her encounter with the old clown Caroline had been under close observation by Hunt. As far as he could tell there had been no discernible change in her demeanor at all. While he was obviously relieved, nevertheless the whole incident still bothered him greatly.

The show concluded a short time later and, for the first time since the audience had first begun to arrive, Hunt began to relax. Then the house lights rose and Hunt stiffened immediately.

What had been obscured by darkness was suddenly crystal clear to him under the cold, neon strip lights. It was
impossibly faint, almost to the point of being invisible, but Hunts preternatural vision still detected its presence. An extremely fine, pulsing red line traced it's way inexorably out of the tent, through the artists exit. Without even checking Hunt was certain of its destination. What concerned him at the moment, however, was its point of origin. Caroline was its source. How this was possible he could not say. Neither could he deny its existence, as much as he may have wished to.

The clean-up was forgotten in favor of more immediate concerns. Hunt began pushing his way through the throng of people trying to exit the tent. His passage through the milling crowd was ungentle and caused more than a few angry stares and muttered expletives to be aimed in his direction. He did not care, so intent was he on his purpose.

As soon as she was close enough, Hunt reached out, taking Caroline forcefully by the arm and pulling her close.

"Joe!" She exclaimed, her face betraying her sudden surprise tinged with an edge of fear. "What are you doing?" She demanded.

It took Hunt a moment to realize just how irrational his actions must have seemed to her. She didn't have his gift. She couldn't see the things he saw. And, in truth, now he was so close to her, he could see no obvious threat.

"I'm sorry." He apologized, releasing his grip on her.

"That really hurt." Caroline cradled her arm to her chest, rubbing the affected area with her free hand. Hunt hung his head.

"I don't know what came over me." He said. It was a lame response, he knew. But how could he possibly explain to her in any way that did not make him appear a raving lunatic?

"I thought I saw something." Was all he could muster in his defense.

Caroline appraised him closely before responding. His face spoke of concern, pure and simple. Concern for her welfare and nothing else. This was a new experience for her. Not since the death of her husband had she felt such a degree of care and attention from another man. It was a little overwhelming, not to say frightening. Yet, at the same time, she found it not at all unpleasant. Finally, she smiled. Warm, open and honest.

"Well whatever it was, you must have scared it off." She said lightly.

"Yeh, I guess so." Hunt was relieved that his ill-conceived actions had not driven her away. Even if she did not realize it, now, more than ever, she needed him nearby.

Caroline moved in closer to Hunt, linking his arm, very much like she had the previous evening.

"Come on." She said gently. "There's a lonely bottle of wine waiting back at the flat. Why don't we give it some company?"

Hunt smiled nervously, but did not refuse. The two exited the tent arm in arm. As they walked back towards Caroline's apartment Hunt gave a backwards glance. There it was, exactly as he had expected. A thin pulsing red line of energy tracing unerringly back to the clowns' caravan.

Chapter 18

They sat in comfortable, metal framed chairs on the balcony in Caroline's apartment, a bottle of dark red Rioja and two heavy crystal glasses on a glass-topped table between them. Caroline spoke intently about her husband, purging the remnants of four years of accumulated grief. For his part, Hunt was content to let her talk, although he listened with only half an ear, his mind working on a more immediate problem.

She didn't seem to notice Hunts' reticence, the flow of words and emotions pouring from her in a steady stream. It was a cathartic process, but one which had a natural end point and, by the time they were halfway through the fine

Rioja it was over. She relaxed back into her chair with a heavy, wistful sigh.

"I don't remember the last time I've talked like that." She concluded with a wan smile.

"It was probably long overdue." Hunt noted.

"I guess it was."

They both silently sipped at their wine, each lost in thoughts of a very different nature. Eventually Caroline placed her empty glass upon the table. She stood and walked around to Hunt, leaning towards him, placing a delicate hand lightly on his shoulder.

"I've had enough excitement for one night Joe. I'm off to bed, are you coming?"

It was a leading question, and Hunt knew it. There was more than sleep on offer here, a lot more. A large part of him desperately wanted to accept, the physical need in him was difficult to ignore, but ignore it he did. Despite a certain amount of renewed confidence following his conversation with Mantle, he still did not trust himself and his ability enough for physical contact, especially contact of so intimate a nature.

"I'll be along in a little while." He said gently.

He noted the look of disappointment on her face. Sighing, he reached up to take her hand, gently enfolding it within his own leather bound fingers, offering as sincere a smile as he could manage.

"Don't be too long then." She said, giving his hand a gentle squeeze before heading off towards the bedroom.

He watched her petit, lithe figure disappear, marveling at his own level of restraint. Before his accident he wouldn't have thought twice about taking the woman to bed only to desert her the next morning if it suited his purpose. It seemed he had undergone changes these past months that went a long way beyond the physical. He wasn't sure how much of a good thing that was.

Pouring himself a fresh glass of wine, Hunt settled back into his chair and began processing the events of the past few days. A surprising amount had happened recently and he really needed to take stock and put everything into some kind of order in his mind.

The unexpected appearance of Mantle had certainly thrown a new twist his way. It did, however, raise a lot of questions. It didn't take a genius to work out that Mantle had been placed into his life, along with the delightfully dangerous Jane, right from the moment he had begun this journey. If the Doc was to be believed then they were here to help him, but help him to do what?

Once more Hunts' thoughts turned to Andrew, his former camera man, returned from the dead, delivering enigmatic messages of some great purpose which Hunt was supposed to fulfill. His ghostly companion had been conspicuous by his absence since Hunt had left him outside of "The Exodus" all those weeks ago. He found himself wondering how long that would continue.

It was with some surprise that Hunt found himself slowly prying his eyes open sometime later. Obviously the wine had had the desired effect and, without even realizing it, he had drifted off to sleep still seated on the balcony. As his mind slowly clawed its way back to consciousness, he wondered what it was that had awoken him. The world was still shrouded in darkness. He guessed the time to be around two o'clock.

"Hello John."

The voice drifted out of the darkness from somewhere
behind him. Hunt turned quickly, drawing a deep, ragged breath as the shock of recognition struck him with a near physical force. Standing before him, with her back to the balcony rail, was a young, golden-haired girl. Hunt knew this girl, her features were indelibly etched into his memory. A hard lump formed in his throat as he remembered vividly the last time he had seen her, over six weeks ago in "The Exodus". Her features then were contorted into a grotesque mask of fear and pain as she had been bound and gagged as a ritual sacrifice. Tears formed in Hunts eyes as he recalled the pleading look upon her young, innocent face. He tried to stand now but his legs would not carry him. He dropped to his knees, fighting to catch his breathe.

"John, you have to calm down." Her soft, delicate voice was filled with concern.

Hunt could not hear her. His mind had retreated back to that terrible moment in the sacrificial chamber. A relentless flashing sequence of images paraded themselves before him. The darkly glistening obsidian blade suspended above the young girls' heart, the wild-eyed, maniacal expression on the face of Julianna as she prepared to commit the bloody deed. The knife flashing downwards, the instant of searing pain as the blade found its' mark and, finally, those deep, vibrant eyes turning cold and dull at the moment of death.

"I am so sorry!" Hunt cried in anguish. He bowed his head unable to look at the young girl. For the first time since that day, John Hunt cried. Great, racking sobs fought their way up from the pit of his stomach. This was a grief the like of which Hunt had never before experienced. All the while, the young girl looked on, her face full of compassion. She glided across the balcony, reaching out a tender, ethereal hand towards Hunts' bowed head.

"It wasn't your fault John."

"I… I failed you." Hunt gasped between sobs.

"No. You did not fail me. It was never your task to save me."

John raised his tear-streaked face, his confusion evident as his grief subsided slightly.

"I don't understand." He confessed.

"Eve was right." The girl said simply. She could see the incredulity forming on Hunts' face. "My fate was decided before I was even born. I was chosen for that moment, and my death was necessary."

"How can you say that?" Hunt demanded.

"Because it is true." She answered simply. "My death provided you with what you needed to destroy Eve. It was required."

"I don't understand."

"I know. That is why I am here, to help you understand."

Hunt sat back on his heels, looking up at the soft gentle features of the young girl standing before him. He noticed now that she wore the same plain white gown as she had on that fateful night, its soft fabric wafting slightly in the gentle summer breeze. Her delicate features no longer bore the pain, anguish and fear he remembered so well, seeming instead to glow with an inner peace. Her sparkling green eyes viewed him with a maturity that went well beyond her years. Looking at her now, Hunt felt the grief slowly draining from him. She
seemed to give off an aura of peace and tranquility that infused everything around her and Hunt felt it washing over him, cleansing him of the pain and deep despair he had felt at

her passing. He drew a deep, relaxing breath and she smiled approvingly.

"You still have no real understanding of what you did that night do you?" She asked, not unkindly. Hunt shook his head.

"I killed Eve, among others." He said bitterly.

"That is true, and in destroying Eve you removed a source of terrible evil from this world. But that was not your only task that night."

Hunts' brow furrowed as he tried to recall all that had occurred.

"The candle?" He said eventually.

"Exactly." She said, obviously pleased that Hunt had made the connection unaided. "The Flame of Ephesus. An ancient and terrible artifact. The flame was a storehouse for virgin souls like mine. As long as the flame burned, the souls contained within the candle were trapped. It was a prison."

"But why?"

"Eve was directly connected to the Flame. She derived her power, her beauty, even her very life from the souls contained within. For centuries she had been performing rituals such as the one you witnessed in order to maintain her collection of souls, thereby ensuring her own immortality."

"And now? The candle is destroyed, so what has happened to all of those souls?"

The young girl smiled.

"Look around you John." She said softly.

The air around the balcony began to shimmer, almost like a summer heat haze. Sparkling silver clouds began to form within the haze, gradually coalescing into distinct figures. Hunt was astounded at the sheer number of them. Hundreds of ethereal young girls appeared before his eyes, not one of them any older than the girl who had been the subject of his nightmares for so long. They seemed to be of every creed and color of the world, their clothing indicative of every period of history one could imagine. Hunt looked on in awe.

"You released them all, John." The young girl said softly. "Thanks to you, they are finally free."

Hundreds of pairs of ghostly eyes looked back at him, each one filled with benevolence and gratitude so intense it was almost overwhelming.

"I know that when you look back on that night John, you see yourself as a murderer. And yes, you did take four lives, that is true. But for each of those four evil souls you banished I can show you a hundred or more pure and gentle souls that you released back into the world."

As one mind each of the young girls mouthed a simple phrase to him. Thank you, they said and then slowly vanished once more. Hunt was left breathless by the extraordinary experience.

"Why haven't you told me this before now?" He asked.

"You were not ready to hear it."

"But now I am?" Hunt thought he understood. He had walked away from Andrew because he was not ready to accept the implications of what he had become, despite, or maybe even because of the events at "The Exodus". Having so
cavalierly dismissed Andrew it was a foregone conclusion that he would never have been prepared to hear what this young girl had to say.

"It is necessary for you to hear it now, John." There was something about her tone that raised alarms.

"What do you mean?" He asked.

"I know what you are hunting. It is a power more dangerous than you could possibly imagine. If you are to have any hope of defeating it then you need to have your mind free of the guilt and grief that has been clouding it these past weeks."

"I see." Hunt said carefully. "Can you tell me anything more specific about this power?"

"I'm sorry, I cannot." Hunt grunted his displeasure. "I can however tell you that you will not be alone in this fight."

"Well that'll make a change." Hunt grunted in a voice heavy with sarcasm.

"Now my time here is done and you need to wake up."

"What?" Hunt was startled. The girl was fading slowly before his eyes.

Looking around he suddenly saw himself, still sleeping in the chair. At first he thought this to be a dream until he heard movement coming from the direction of the living room. As disconcerting as it was, Hunt disregarded the sight of his still slumbering form, glancing instead through the open doorway which led into the apartment.

"Hurry John." The young girl urged, her voice now barely above a whisper. "You don't have much time."

He saw Caroline walking from the coffee table towards the
hallway and the front door. She was fully dressed and carried a set of car keys in her right hand. They jangled softly as she moved.

"Caroline!" He called to her.

"She cannot hear you." The young girl whispered to him. "You must wake. Now!!"

Hunt looked back at his body, looking so peaceful on the balcony chair. He closed his eyes and willed himself to wake. The last thing he heard was the faintest whisper of the girls' voice just on the edge of hearing.

"Know this John. If you fall, I will catch you."

Then his eyes opened.

Chapter 19

There was a short period of disorientation as Hunt adjusted his perspective. Shaking his head to clear away the cobwebs he stood, a little unsteadily, turning towards the front door just in time to see it close, the latch clicking back into place with a dull thunk. Caroline was gone.

"Shit." He exclaimed, moving quickly to follow.

He was operating now on a purely instinctive level. Whatever destination Caroline had in mind, Hunt knew, with a cold certainty that he had to prevent her reaching it at all costs. With an urgency that set his blood to pounding he raced to the apartment door, bursting through it into the stairwell.

Caroline was already nearing the ground floor. Taking the stairs two at a time, Hunt bounded after her calling her name as he went.

"Caroline!" He shouted, heedless of the noise he was making at so early an hour. She gave no indication that she had heard him, continuing on her path out of the building without a pause.

Hunt crashed through the buildings main exit with such force that the door rattled dangerously in its frame.

By now Caroline had already reached her car, an aged blue Volvo, and was unlocking the drivers' door. There was no sense of urgency about her movements, they were calm and unhurried.

"Caroline, stop!" Hunt shouted again. Still no response. Hunt had made enough noise now that a number of lights were coming on in the building. Disgruntled residents, rudely awoken from their slumber, would soon be looking for someone to blame for the disturbance. Hunt didn't care. He broke into a run as Caroline, continuing to ignore his pleas, calmly climbed into her vehicle, closing the door behind her.

Hunts' progress was brought to an abrupt and surprising halt by the sudden appearance of the man, stepping calmly out of the shadows directly into his path.

"Good morning Mr. Hunt." The man said pleasantly. "You are Mr. John Hunt, aren't you?"

Hunt looked at the man in astonishment. He was tall, well-dressed in a three piece suit, his manner relaxed and confident.

"Who the hell are you?" Hunt demanded crossly, eyes darting between the interloper and Caroline's car which was even now backing out of its parking space.

"Detective Inspector Cunningham, Bath police. I need to have a word with you Mr. Hunt."

"Bath police?" Hunt said in amazement. "I don't have time for this." He tried to brush past the man, only to find himself restrained, his arm held fast in a surprisingly powerful grip.

"I think I'm going to have to insist." Cunningham said in a low, dangerous tone.

"Let go of me." Hunt snatched his arm free in a sudden burst of strength, even as the dark Volvo began to pull off the parking area.

"Caroline! Stop!" Hunt screamed, trying in vain to get past the irritating figure that continued to block his path.

He was forced to watch helplessly as Caroline continued on her way, turning left onto the main street and driving into the distance.

"God damn it!" Hunt screamed in frustration.

"You need to calm down." Cunningham said.

"Shut the fuck up!" Hunt snapped. "I could have stopped her you fucking idiot. But no, you had to get in the way. Jesus Christ!"

Cunningham was doing his best to conceal his bemusement at this strange turn of events. He had arrived in Eastbourne several hours earlier, having decided to track Agent Mantle down for himself. By the time he had located the circus ground, the show had long since finished and there were few people left to question. As expected, they were a relatively close-mouthed group, but he had found one or two willing to answer some questions.

Mantle was unknown to them but Hunts picture yielded surprising results. The apartment block had been indicated as a possible location for Hunt but no-one could tell him any more than that.

Having nothing better to do, and not wanting to take the
chance of losing Hunt, the Detective had parked up in the car park and was planning on waiting to catch Hunt in the morning.

Cunningham had considered a variety of scenarios for how their encounter would play out, none of which matched the one he currently found himself enacting. Hunt was not reacting in anything like the expected fashion. He was pacing back and forth, muttering angrily to himself and virtually ignoring the Detective. When Hunt did glance in his direction, it was with a look of such withering scorn that Cunningham almost felt offended.

He had expected Hunt to be at least moderately fearful, that was how most people reacted when suddenly confronted with a police detective. Hunt, however, resolutely refused to co-operate. Rather than being fearful of Cunningham, he treated him almost as an inconvenience, an irritation. This was not a reaction Cunningham was used to getting and he really didn't know how to respond to it.

It was clear that the Detective had stepped into the middle of something and, whatever it was, it had seriously rattled Hunt. None of that mattered however. Cunningham needed answers and Hunt was the only one who could provide them. It was time he exerted his authority.

"Ok Mr. Hunt, I need you to come with me."

Hunt stopped his pacing, turning to glare at the Detective. His face creased in thought as he stepped forwards towards the wary officer.

"You have a car here?" He asked suddenly.

"Of course." Cunningham answered slowly.

"Good. Then here's the deal. I'll go with you. I'll answer all of your questions. But first, I need you to help me."

"This isn't a negotiation." Cunningham, said sharply.

"Listen Detective." Hunt spat, his face a mask of barely restrained fury. "That woman that just left here, the one you stopped me reaching, she is going to die tonight unless I can do something to stop it. Now you have a choice. You can either continue to get in my way, in which case you become partly responsible for her death. Alternatively you can help me and maybe, just maybe, we have a chance of saving her. What's it to be."

Cunningham was taken aback by this sudden ultimatum.

"What the hell is going on?" He blustered.

"I don't have time to explain." Hunt said firmly. "Stay or go. It's your choice, but make it now."

The Detective was at a loss. He didn't know if he really believed Hunt but, it was clear that events had happened over the course of the past few days about which he had no rational explanation, and all of these events somehow connected to the man standing before him. What finally made the decision for him was the look on Hunts face. There was no hint of deception to be found. While Cunningham wasn't entirely sure that he believed Hunts' desperate claim it was abundantly clear that Hunt did. Under these circumstances the Detective simply did not feel he could take the risk.

"Follow me."

"Thank you." Hunt said as he followed after the rapidly moving Cunningham.

The Detective led Hunt to a plain-looking, silver, two-door Ford Focus, an old, but a reliable car. Cunningham was already starting the engine as Hunt climbed into the passenger seat.

"I suppose you know where she's going then?"

Hunt paused in the act of putting his seat belt on. Until now he hadn't actually thought about her destination. He was about to admit that he did not know when a thought occurred to him. It was so obvious that he doubted it could possibly be correct but, having no other information to work with he decided to take a chance.

"Beachy Head." He said simply.

"If you say so." Cunningham responded, the doubt evident in his voice.

As a Detective, Cunningham wasn't too concerned with such things as speed limits so, with tires squealing in protest, he spun rapidly off the parking area in pursuit of the old Volvo.

Despite the fact that the Volvo had such a big head start on them, Cunningham felt confident that he could catch up with it, always assuming they were headed in the right direction.

He glanced across at his passenger. Anxiety, frustration, concern were all evident on Hunts' face. Cunningham shook his head in confusion. One thing was certain, Hunt fitted none of the murder profiles Cunningham had ever read.

"Feel like telling me what's going on?" He ventured, Hunt snorted derisively.

"You'd never believe me."

"You don't know unless you try." Cunningham responded in a reasonable tone. "I might surprise you."

"Please. Just drive." Hunt said shortly.

They drove on in silence. At this early hour the roads remained virtually clear and Cunningham was able to speed through the streets without too much effort. It was not too long before they found themselves upon the main coast road that led out towards Beachy Head.

All the while Cunningham was trying to comprehend what was happening. So far he had two young boys in Bath, dead. Brutally murdered in a manner he could not explain.

The MI5 Agent who had taken the case from him was now missing under circumstances which went well beyond suspicious. Now, there was a young woman in Eastbourne whose life was apparently in grave danger. All that connected these three elements together was John Hunt, but for the life of him, Cunningham could not work out how. He felt like he was trying to put a jigsaw puzzle together when he had never seen the final image. He had no context, no framework to guide him. It was frustrating beyond measure.

For his part, Hunt was focused entirely upon the plight that Caroline was now in. Ever since her unexplained departure from the apartment he had begun to suspect the truth. The choice of Beachy Head as a destination was an instinctive one. He hoped that he was wrong.

Cunningham threw the Ford around yet another bend in the winding road. As he straightened the vehicle Hunt saw twin pools of light in the distance.

"Slow down." He said softly.

The Detective had seen the same lights but did not appreciate their importance. The cars' speed dropped gradually to a more sedate pace as they drew closer to the lights. They illuminated a lay-by on the left side of the road.

Hunt sighed in resignation. It was as he had feared. The Volvo was roughly parked lengthwise across the lay-by, lights still on and the drivers' door open. Of Caroline there was no sign.

Hunt was fumbling with his seat belt even before the Detective brought his own vehicle to a jarring halt behind the Volvo. The instant they had stopped Hunt was out of the car and racing across the fields towards the cliff.

Cunningham followed more slowly. He didn't have to be a Detective to understand what was happening here. As he swiftly scanned ahead, he was filled with a deep sense of foreboding.

"Caroline!" Hunt called desperately.

He could see her approaching the cliffs edge. There was no possible way he could reach her in time, this he knew, yet still he ran.

She had stopped now and each step brought Hunt closer to her. For the briefest of moments he thought he might make it in time. Then, with barely a pause, she stepped forwards and dropped out of sight.

"Caroline!!" Hunt screamed again, his voice cracking as the horror of the moment swept over him. He was running so fast that he almost followed in Caroline's wake. In truth, he wanted to, if only to bring an end to the gut-wrenching pain that threatened to tear his chest apart. But, he didn't. Skidding to a stop with barely a foot to spare, Hunt found himself staring downwards towards the base of the cliff. There was nothing to see, however, darkness obscured all.

Cunningham was in a state of mild shock, having witnessed all. It was clear Hunt had known along that this was what the young woman had intended to do. The question was how he had known. He approached the immobile Hunt slowly from the rear, taking a firm hold of his arm.

"Come on Mr. Hunt." He said, not without sympathy. "There's nothing we can do here."

"Let me go." Hunt said in a low, toneless voice.

"You know I can't do that. We need to get the authorities out here."

"I said.." Hunts' voice was firmer. "Let, me, GO!"

Cunningham never saw it coming. Spinning on his heel, Hunt lashed out. All of the anger, frustration and pain that had built up in him went into a single, focused punch. It connected squarely on the Detectives' jaw, lifting him off his feet and depositing him in a crumpled heap several feet away.

Hunt flexed his hand a few times, wincing slightly at the stinging sensation. He welcomed the physical pain, it provided a much needed distraction from the profound emptiness he now felt inside.

He turned back to look down over the cliff edge, the recumbent police officer temporarily forgotten. The pervading darkness still obscured everything below but, as he watched, his altered vision began to detect something unusual occurring within the darkness.

Hunt watched in fascination as, far below, a deep red cloud began to form. It pulsed and undulated in much the same fashion as the energy aura Hunt had seen around the old clown. As he watched, the cloud began to rise.

It rose steadily, all the while pulsing with its deep, red glow. Reaching the top of the cliff the cloud continued to climb higher. Arcing over

Hunts' head, the cloud moved to a distance of no more than a few feet where it stopped, hovering in place. Hunt was mesmerized, enthralled. He found himself holding his breath in anticipation, wondering what would happen next. He did not have to wait long to find out.

Without warning, the cloud lowered itself slowly, drawing itself into a funnel shape as it did so, its' point touching the ground in front of Hunt. He moved closer cautiously as the cloud began to diminish in size. It was as if it was being drawn into the very earth itself. Hunt reached it just as the final wisps were disappearing. Kneeling down, he saw that it was not the ground that had drawn the cloud, as he had first thought.

Lying, barely visible amongst the grass was a small, wooden disc, about the size of a two pound coin. It was fashioned of some dark wood and it pulsed with a familiar red glow. The glow began to diminish and the air around the wooden disk started to shimmer. Unbelievably, the disk itself began to fade. The disk was disappearing.

Without even thinking about it, Hunt reached out, making a grab for the disk. There was a moment of intense pain as his hand seemed to cross through some invisible barrier. Hunt gritted his teeth and fought through the pain until his fingers finally closed around the now ethereal form of the disk. There was a brief, blinding flash followed by a crackle of something akin to static electricity, then nothing. The pain had ceased almost immediately. Hunt opened his hand revealing the plain disk of wood, as solid as it ever was, a dull red glow pulsating gently around it.

"Interesting." Was all Hunt could think to say.

He stood and slowly walked back to the cliffs edge. The sun was just starting to rise now and, looking down once more, Hunt could just make out Caroline's broken and battered form sprawled upon the rocks below. He sighed with a deep, profound regret.

"I am so sorry Caroline." He said softly, his words being carried swiftly away on the rising sea breeze. "I couldn't stop them from harming you, from taking you." His face hardened then, becoming cold, devoid of all emotion, while his right hand tightened its grip upon the tiny wooden disk, the leather gloves stretched so tight they actually creaked in protest. "But I can make sure they harm no-one else." He promised resolutely.

Chapter 20

Mantle arrived at the circus ground just after eight o'clock that same morning, bringing his sleek Jaguar to a smooth halt on the neighboring car park. He was surprised to find Hunt waiting for him already. There were a couple of wooden picnic tables standing at one edge of the car park. Hunt was sitting on one such table now, his feet resting on the accompanying wooden bench, gaze fixed outwards, across the field in the direction of the circus tent. He showed no indication that he was even aware of Mantles' arrival as the former Doctor approached, feet crunching loudly on the gravel topped parking area.

"Good morning." Mantle greeted brightly.

"Caroline's dead." Hunt grunted his tone flat, devoid of emotion.

Mantle stopped, facing Hunt. He looked the man over, noting the tired, worn look on the younger mans' face. It was clear Hunt had not slept. Mantle was aware of his encounter with the young woman, Caroline. Hunt had mentioned her during their conversation the previous day. Her death had obviously had a profound effect on him now. Hoisting himself up with only a few grunts, mantle took a seat next to Hunt on the picnic table.

"Tell me what happened."

Taking a deep breath, Hunt began to relate the events of the previous night. Mantle listened attentively, all the while analyzing Hunts' body language. His shoulders were slumped, a result of tiredness, certainly, but there was something more. His flat, even monotone delivery of his tale spoke of a lack of emotion that Mantle found more than a little disturbing.

The appearance of the Detective had taken Mantle by surprise and he paused Hunts' narration in order to question him in more detail about this unexpected turn of events.

"What did you say his name was?" Mantle quizzed.

"Detective Inspector Cunningham. He said he was from Bath."

"How on earth did he track you here?" Mantle mused, his brow creasing with thought.

"You can ask him yourself when he wakes up."

"What do you mean? Where is he?"

Hunt nodded in the direction of the silver Ford Focus parked several feet away. Mantle had not previously taken much note of the car. He squinted slightly now, noting the shadow of a person, apparently slumped in the passenger seat of the vehicle.

"What happened to him?"

"He got in my way" Hunt answered simply.

Mantle shook his head.

"John." It was surprising how much disapproval he managed to squeeze into that single word.

"He didn't give me a choice." Hunt offered by way of explanation.

"Fine. I'll deal with him in a few moments. You'd better tell me the rest of it, John?"

Hunt ploughed onwards with his tale. He described the pursuit, their arrival at Beachy Head and Caroline's ultimate suicide. It was only then that Hunt developed a slight catch in his voice. Mantle felt a great sympathy for the man at that moment. He hated forcing him to relive those terrible moments, but it was necessary.

At the point when Hunt began describing the strange cloud, Mantles' interest was especially piqued. He listened carefully, closing his eyes in order to better visualize the descriptions Hunt provided. For his part, Hunt continued in his disturbingly efficient monotone, relating the sequence of events almost as if her were a passive observer rather than someone who was intimately, and emotionally, involved in the proceedings.

"And do you still have this disk?" Mantle asked once his companion had reached the end of his strange tale.

Slowly, Hunt withdrew the small wooden disk, holding it out in the palm of his hand for Mantle to examine. The old man drew closer, scrutinizing the plain dark circle.

"It doesn't look like much, does it?" He observed eventually.

"So, do you know what we're dealing with?" Hunt asked. Mantle shrugged.

"I might. But, before we get to that I think I'd better go and deal with our new friend over there."

Hunt glanced in the direction of the Focus. The dark shape was beginning to stir.

"You wait here please John." Mantle said, climbing down off the picnic table. He began to walk towards the car when Hunt called out to him.

"Doc!" Mantle turned back. "You might need this." Hunt said, tossing something in the old mans' direction. Mantle caught the object easily. Holding it up, he saw that it was a small key, the kind one used on a set of handcuffs. He gave Hunt a questioning look.

"It seemed like the thing to do at the time." Hunt offered casually. Shaking his head, Mantle continued towards the vehicle.

For Detective Inspector Cunningham the day was not starting off very well at all. As the slow march back to consciousness had begun he proceeded to take stock of his situation, several points of interest clamored for attention.

First and foremost was the intense pain along his jawline. As the fog cleared in his brain the Detective tried to recall the events that had led him here. He remembered Hunt, the drive, the cliffs and then, blackness. Cunningham had never been struck so hard in his entire life. He flexed his jaw, wincing at the fire that spread up through the side of his face. At least it didn't seem to be broken.

Looking down, he saw the state of his clothing. The fine three piece suit that was his pride and joy was crumpled,
creased and covered in dirt. This level of disarray was an anathema to a man of his fastidious nature. Then he noticed the handcuffs.

Looped through the passenger side doorhandle, they proved a very effective restraint. Knowing it was a futile exercise, Cunningham pulled on them anyway. He strained against the door for several seconds, the pain in his wrists as the cold metal of the cuffs dug mercilessly into the skin eventually forcing him to stop.

"Damn." He cursed in frustration.

It was at this point that the drivers-side door opened and Mantle stepped inside, taking time to make himself comfortable behind the wheel.

"Ah Detective." He greeted the man with a warm smile. "You're awake then? Good."

"Get these damn things off me!" Cunningham growled, indicating the cuffs that bound his wrists.

"All in good time." Mantle said leaning forward to place the handcuff key on the dashboard between them. "I think we need to have a conversation first."

There was silence for a moment as the two men eyed each other carefully. Eventually, Cunningham relaxed back into the passenger seat, staring resolutely out of the windscreen, his face set into a stony mask.

"I assume you know who I am?" Mantle asked.

"Yes." The Detective responded curtly. Mantle nodded.

"Good. Of course it goes without saying that I know who you are. What I don't know, and what I would really like to know is, how you managed to track us here."

"Your colleague, Agent D'Arcy."

"Interesting." Mantle murmured softly. "I'm going to need more than that I'm afraid."

With some reluctance, Cunningham relayed the events that had brought him to Eastbourne. His manner was abrupt, yet surprisingly detailed and it wasn't long before Mantle had a clear picture laid out before him.

"So I take it this little excursion of yours was not exactly sanctioned by your station chief?" Mantle observed astutely.

"No" Cunningham admitted.

"I see. And Agent D'Arcy? Have you had any more information regarding her whereabouts?"

"No. I haven't had a chance to check in with anyone since I arrived."

"Well, we'll have to put that to one side for now." Mantle said, Cunningham detected a slight catch to the older mans' voice.

"You're worried about her." He stated.

"Not really, no." Mantle lied. "That's one girl who is a lot tougher than she looks."

Cunningham knew that Mantle was lying and Mantle knew that Cunningham knew he was lying, yet neither man decided to voice their thoughts on the matter.

"So what happens now?" Cunningham asked.

"Well, that largely depends upon you Detective. Tell me, are you a religious or spiritual man?"

The question caught the Detective off guard. He was unsure as to its relevance, yet an examination of the older mans' face told him that Mantle considered it to be important.

"On balance, I'd have to say no." Cunningham said eventually. Mantle pursed his lips thoughtfully.

"Perhaps that's no bad thing." He said, taking the single key of the dashboard and reaching across the Detective. "Detective Cunningham," He continued. "Your size tens have stomped their way right into the middle of something you may not be intellectually equipped to deal with." There was a soft click as the first cuff released. Mantle handed the key over to the Detective who proceeded to release his second wrist, a look of displeasure on his face. "I mean no disrespect Detective." Mantle continued. "Quite the opposite, in fact. I believe you could be useful to my team."

Cunningham frowned slightly.

"What do you mean, useful?" He asked suspiciously.

"I'm prepared to give you an opportunity to see this case through to its natural conclusion, wherever that may lead. But, if I am to do that, I first need to know that you will keep an open mind. Can you do that?"

The question hung in the air between them. Cunningham was not entirely sure what the old man was talking about. He did, however, recognize a potential opportunity when he saw it. There was also the matter of Hunt. Instinctively, the Detective knew that the man was central to everything that was happening. A Detective through and through, Cunningham had to know how this picture pieced together. Ultimately there was only one answer he could give and, he suspected, Mantle already knew this.

"I can do that." He said finally. Mantle smiled.

"Good." He reached into his pocket and withdrew a set of
car keys. "My car is over there." He indicated the Jaguar with a nod of his head. "You'll find a packet of pain killers in the glove compartment

and a bottle of water in the seat well. Come and join us when you're ready."

Hunt had barely moved, Mantle noted as he exited the Focus. The young man remained much as Mantle had left him, staring resolutely out towards the circus tent, his face blank of emotion. Mantle did not need Hunts' unique ability to see auras for him to be aware of the heavy air of gloom that hung over his younger companion. The death of the young girl, Caroline, had obviously affected him deeply. Mantle was concerned. After everything Hunt had experienced and endured over the past few weeks, would this latest event prove to be too much for his already battered psyche? Only time would tell.

"How is he?" Hunt asked as Mantle approached.

"He'll recover." Mantle answered. "Although I do think you owe him an apology. That's quite a bruise you left on him." Hunt shrugged disinterestedly.

"What's next?" Hunt asked, directing Mantles' thoughts back to their immediate situation.

"Well, based on what you've told me, I think I know what we are dealing with, but I need to know more if I am to be sure."

"Fine, then let's go to the source?" Hunt asked softly.

Mantle followed the direction of Hunts' gaze. He was just in time to see two men, one obviously much older than the other, disappearing into the tent via the artists' entrance. A slow smile crept across his face.

Chapter 21

"It's no good, Dad. It's not here."

The two men, Father and Son, were both searching the ground around the center seating section. Both holding hand-held torches, the father was bent over, playing the torch light over the grassy ground beneath the seats while his son was on his hands and knees, making a much closer examination of the same area.

"It has to be here." The fathers' deep voice growled desperately.

"Looking for something gentlemen?"

Both men jumped in surprise, turning to face the source of the unexpected question.

Hunt stood squarely in the center of the ring, his cold, impassive face watching them intensely. On the one side stood Detective Cunningham, looking only slightly disheveled now in his moderately crumpled three-piece. Mantle stood on Hunts' second flank, his posture relaxed, a slight smirk curling his lips. It was he who had voiced the question.

"What are you doing here?" The old man asked, being the first to recover his composure. "You need to leave. Now!"

"Oh, I don't think so." Mantle responded glibly.

"Now wait a minute…" The old man began angrily. His sons' hand on his arm stopped him in mid-flow.

"Dad!" The younger clown breathed softly. "Look." He pointed towards Hunt.

Cunningham knew he was little more than an observer at the moment. He had absolutely no idea what was going on. Hunt had been standing silently at his side, idly rolling the wooden disk back and forth across the knuckles of his right hand. The Detective was surprised at the reaction this engendered from the old man. A range of emotions played quickly across the fathers' face, settling finally on two, surprise and fear. They seemed to battle for supremacy with neither gaining any ground. Cunningham wondered what was so special about this simple, plain piece of wood.

"That doesn't belong to you." The old man said dangerously. Hunt grabbed at the disk suddenly, clenching it firmly in the palm of his hand.

"You could try and take it back." Hunt said evenly. "But I wouldn't recommend that."

There was something about the way that Hunt said it that gave the old man pause. He squinted slightly, as he made a closer examination of Hunts' face.

"I know you." He said suddenly. "You're Joe. You work here. Look, I don't think you understand what you've got there."

"We understand better than you think." Mantle said confidently. "Would you like me to tell you a little story about it?" Mantle began walking forwards slowly as he spoke. "It's a simple little tale. A young woman goes to see a circus one night. She has fun, it's a good show. But she didn't know that she had been singled out by a certain old, overweight clown who happened to be very good at sleight of hand. When she left the show that night, she had no idea that she was taking a little gift with her. This gift caused her to drive out to the coast in the dead of night and throw herself off a cliff." Mantle paused. He was standing right next to the old man. Leaning in closer, he whispered into the old clowns' ear. "Does any of this sound familiar?"

"Her name was Caroline." Hunt added coldly.

Throughout the monologue, the old Clown had remained impassive but, at the mention of the girls' name his face dropped, features etched with pain and guilt.

"I'm sorry." He said in a voice near to breaking.

"Dad, what are you saying?" His son, jumped up running to his fathers' side.

"It doesn't matter anymore, Son. Listen to them. They already know. "

"Excuse me." Cunningham interjected suddenly. "Are you saying you are somehow responsible for this woman's death?"

"Not exactly Detective." Mantle interrupted quickly. "They are responsible for arranging the circumstances that led to her death. That's correct isn't it?"

"Yes?" The old man breathed.

Cunningham shook his head in confusion.

"This makes no sense at all." He stated bluntly.

"Remember what I said about keeping an open mind Detective?" Mantle admonished gently before turning back to the old man. "I need you to tell me everything."

The old man turned away, head bowed, whether from tiredness or shame Hunt could not tell. In truth, he did not care. His capacity for sympathy at this point was virtually nil.

"Where to begin." The old man mused, taking a seat on the front row, his son occupying the seat next to him and to his right. Mantle crouched down before the old man. He displayed openly the sympathy that Hunt could not feel.

""This has been a part of our family for as long as I can remember. A curse I suppose you'd call it."

"Go on." Mantle urged.

"It comes to me in my dreams, tells me what to do, and I have to obey it."

"What does?" Hunt asked sharply. Mantle gave his younger companion a pointed look.

"I don't know. I never see it, just, hear its voice, in my head. I never knew you could hear evil."

"Only you can hear it?" Mantle asked. The old man nodded.

"Yes. It was my father before me, and his father before him. And when I die….." He looked over towards his son, despair filling his eyes.

"I see." Mantle said softly.

"And what about this?" Hunt asked, holding out the wooden disk.

"That comes from the mirror." The old man said. "A family heirloom."

"Ahhh." Mantle breathed. "That's what I needed to know. I think we need to take a look at this mirror. Do you mind?"

Without a doubt, this was the strangest case Cunningham had ever investigated. He couldn't imagine what a mirror could have to do with anything, but, having been soundly admonished once already by the ageing MI5 Agent, the Detective decided to tag along without protest as they all trouped back to the clowns' caravan.

Despite its obvious age, the interior of the caravan was surprisingly clean, tidy and extremely well-appointed. A main seating and dining area lay at the front end while the large, master bedroom was at the rear. Its center was taken up by a well-designed galley kitchen, small single bedroom and even shower and toilet facilities. It was towards the master bedroom that the old man directed them now.

"The mirror's in there."

"Thank you," Mantle said. "Why don't you all take a seat here while I have a look." He suggested. "John, would you accompany me please?"

While the two clowns and Cunningham took seats on opposite sides of the fold-down dining table, Mantle headed towards the master bedroom, with Hunt only a step behind him.

The bedroom was just as neat and ordered as the rest of the caravan. A large double bed was freshly made with plain white sheets and a single pillow at the head. There was very little by way of personal effects within the room.

"What do you think, John?" Mantle asked, indicating the large, oval mirror that hung by a heavy-looking chain from the wardrobe door to the side of the bed. The wooden frame was of the same dark wood as the disc Hunt still held. At the top of the oval there was a circular hole in the wood. Hunt knew with a certainty that the dimensions of the hole would exactly match with those of the disc.

That wasn't, however, what Mantle had meant. The old man had wanted to know what Hunts' altered vision could determine. And the simple answer to that question was, a lot.

For Hunt, the entire room was bathed in a dull, red glow that writhed and pulsed disturbingly. The glow emanated from the mirror. That much was clear. However, there was something else. The frame was crisscrossed with what appeared to be a web of silver-white glowing filaments. Similar in look and hue to the normal aura he perceived around people, only in this case, they were far more intense. He had no idea what it all meant but, he diligently reported his findings in as much detail as he could.

"Is this what you expected?" Hunt asked.

"Suspected would be a better word." Mantle answered softly. "In all truth, I'd hoped I was wrong."

"You know what this is then?

"Oh I do indeed." Mantle confirmed.

"Good. Then you know how to destroy it."

"That is exactly the problem, my boy." Mantle said seriously. "I'm not entirely sure it can be destroyed."

Chapter 22

Cunningham noted the looks on the faces of both men as they returned from the master bedroom. A sense of gloom seemed to hang above them. While he did not entirely understand what was happening at the moment, it was clear that something needed to be done to lighten the mood, even if only a little.

"Well, I don't know about anyone else, but I could use a drink." He stood, motioning for the two men to take a seat. "Why don't I put the kettle on?" He continued brightly. Mantle threw him a grateful smile.

"That sounds like a wonderful idea." He agreed. "You don't mind, do you?" He asked the old clown.

"Please, make yourselves at home." He nudged his son in the ribs. "Go and help the man Sean."

As the younger clown joined Cunningham in the galley kitchen, Mantle looked across at his father.

"Tell me about the mirror then"

"There's not much to tell." The old man confessed miserably. "Like I said, it's been in the family for as long as I can remember. Where we got it from originally, I don't know."

"What do you know about it Doc?" Hunt asked suddenly. Mantle took a deep breath before answering.

"Quite a lot actually." Mantle confessed. "What do you know of the Grimaldi family?" He asked of the group.

"Even I've heard of them." Cunningham piped in from the galley.

"Aren't you supposed to be related to them somehow?" Hunt asked the old clown.

"Well, it's part of the sales pitch." The old man admitted depreciatingly. "Honestly though, I don't know how much truth there is to it."

"The fact that you have that mirror tells me that you are definitely related somehow." Mantle stated. Hunt snorted angrily.

"Enough with the hints Doc." He snapped. "What do you know about that damned mirror?"

Cunningham frowned at this sudden outburst. He had been quietly observing the interactions between Hunt and the old MI5 Agent all morning. There was a curious relationship developing between the two men. The Detective had naturally assumed that Mantle would be in charge, now he was not so sure.

"Fine." Mantle said with a long sigh. "The mirror is almost two hundred years old. It was made in 1825 by a master craftsman of the time who possessed some rather unique skills
and it was created specifically for the Grimaldi family or, more accurately Joseph Samuel William Grimaldi, the son of the famous Joseph Grimaldi."

"I'm grim all day, so you can laugh all night." The old clown said suddenly. Mantle nodded.

"Grimaldis' catch phrase, yes." Mantle said sadly. "Unfortunately, unknown to their audience, that phrase proved to be more than an amusing play on words. Off-stage, the Grimaldi family led desperately unhappy lives, beset by misfortune."

Cunningham, with help from the younger clown, Sean, delivered their drinks at that moment. Mantle took a long drink of the steaming liquid with a grateful smile.

"Thank you." He said.

"So what happened to the Grimaldi family then?" The Detective asked, surprisingly interested in the story.

"Well, I could spend all day regaling their tale of woe. Suffice to say that not one of their lives ended well. What is important from our point of view is that their misfortune was no random quirk of fate. It was artificially generated by an outside source."

"Ok, now you've lost me." Cunningham confessed.

"An external and extremely malevolent entity known as the Cloyne had taken control of their lives, manipulating them and everything around them to its own ends."

"Malevolent entity?" Cunningham asked skeptically. Mantle noted the Detectives' tone and shot him another warning look.

"You would call the Cloyne a demon." He clarified. "An ancient and powerful creature that draws its energy from the despair of others. It feeds off humanities darkest fears and emotions, pain, loss, grief."

"And you're saying this thing was feeding off the Grimaldi family?" Sean asked. "Making their lives so terrible so that it could have, what? A feast?"

"Essentially yes." Mantle affirmed.

"Sounds like one of Grimms' fairy tales if you ask me." Cunningham said sourly.

"I won't tell you again Mr. Cunningham." Mantle stated sternly. Cunningham shook his head.

"Look, I'm sorry, but this is just not possible. I mean, what are we talking about here? Demons? Really? It's utter nonsense in my opinion."

"Mr. Cunningham. When you have had the benefit of witnessing one tenth of the things I have seen in this world then, perhaps, you may be in a position to offer an opinion as to what is and is not possible. Until then, I'll thank you to be quiet."

Cunningham held up his hands in a placating gesture. He knew he had stepped well over the line. All of this talk of demons was little more than outrageous fantasy. Still, he did not take Mantle for a fool and it was clear that the MI5 agent fully believed in what he was saying. Despite himself, the Detective was secretly intrigued by all of this.

"How does all of this connect to the mirror?" Hunt asked.

"Well, if you remember I said that the craftsman who made this mirror had some "unique skills"?" Mantle answered. As he said this he looked pointedly in Hunts' direction, making it perfectly clear to the younger man what kind of skills he meant.

Hunt frowned thoughtfully. This meant that there had been others who had "acquired" skills of a similar nature to his own. If that were true then it gave rise to a whole series of questions, questions Hunt desperately wanted to ask. But he restrained himself. This wasn't the time for any kind of personal exploration. For the moment at least, Hunt put those questions aside, confident in the knowledge that, at some point in the not too distant future there would be a better opportunity for Mantle and himself to explore them at their leisure.

"It was no accident that this Craftsman encountered the Grimaldi family." Mantle continued. "He had been searching for this demon, The Cloyne, for some time."

"He was some sort of Demon Hunter then?" Cunningham asked.

"If you like." Mantle confirmed. "The term fits as well as any other."

"So why didn't he destroy this thing then?" Cunningham pressed.

"He couldn't." Mantle answered simply. "You have to understand that this creature had been gorging itself for years off the despair of the Grimaldi family. By the time it was discovered it was far too powerful for the Craftsman to destroy, so he did the next best thing."

"He imprisoned it." Hunt guessed. "That mirror was created specifically to contain the demon."

"Quite."

"All of that is very interesting." Sean, the younger clown declared. "But it doesn't explain why it has affected my family for so long, or even how."

"The why is very simple." Mantle responded. "The craftsman needed help in order to capture the demon and trap it within the mirror. He found that help in the form of Joseph Grimaldi junior."

"The man was bait for the trap?" Cunningham offered.

"Exactly." Mantle said, obviously pleased that the Detective had offered a positive contribution to the discussion. "Unfortunately that act forever bound the demon to the Grimaldi blood line."

"Ok," Sean's father said slowly. "But, if I remember correctly, didn't the son die shortly after that?"

"Also correct, seven years later to be precise."

"There's no record of him ever having children so the blood line ended with him." The old clown persisted.

"That's not entirely true." Mantle observed. "The Grimaldi bloodline is actually far murkier than most people believe. Joseph Grimaldi Junior died young and childless, true. The bloodline, however did not end with him. Joseph Grimaldi Senior had a brother, John Baptiste, who signed on a ship as a cabin boy and changed his name. Also Giuseppe Grimaldi, Joseph Seniors' father, was known to have sired several children with various women. So you see, there is a very real possibility that your family can trace its' lineage back to one of those elements of the Grimaldi bloodline."

"So, once Joseph Grimaldi Junior died the demon simply transferred its connection to another member of the bloodline." Hunt mused.

"That's essentially it, yes." Mantle confirmed.

"But how could it do that if it's still imprisoned." Sean asked.

"Because the prison is faulty." Hunt answered flatly. "The craftsman made a mistake.

Not only was he not strong enough to destroy the creature. He wasn't strong enough to contain it either."

"That does seem to be the case." Mantle agreed sadly.

"It can't break free." Hunt continued slowly. "But it has enough power to enable it to influence those closest to it, those with a connection to it."

"You mean us." The old clown said morosely.

"Yes." Hunt confirmed. His mind was working rapidly as he put the remaining pieces of the puzzle together. "You are its instruments in this world. You do its bidding, finding new victims for it. People who are suffering, grieving, in despair, all potential food sources. You give them this." He pulled the wooden disc out of his pocket. "This is part of the mirror and it provides a conduit between the victim and the demon. The Cloyne uses this conduit to influence their dreams, heightening their anxieties to a point where the victim feels they have no choice but to commit suicide. Then, at the point of death, all of that energy which is released is collected in this disc which the

Cloyne then retrieves." Hunt suddenly realized that everyone was watching him intently. He blushed a little. "At least, that's what I think anyway."

"I think you're right." Mantle conceded, no small amount of surprise in his voice. "The question is, what do we do now?"

"Destroy the mirror." Cunningham said simply. Hunt shook his head.

"We can't. The energy used to create the prison and contain the demon also serves to protect the mirror itself from all forms of physical harm."

"Besides," Mantle added. "I strongly suspect that destroying the mirror would only serve to release the demon, and that really wouldn't do."

"You said the prison was faulty." Sean said to Hunt. "Can't it be repaired?"

Mantle looked at Hunt, his expression hopeful. Hunt shook his head firmly.

"I wouldn't even know where to start." He admitted.

"Well if we can't repair it and we can't destroy it, what else is there?" The old clown asked desperately.

"I think there is another option." Hunt said slowly, the thought still forming in his mind. "The Cloyne didn't get fed last night. I stopped that."

"How did you manage that by the way?" Cunningham asked.

"I'm not entirely sure." Hunt confessed. "But I think that I am connected to this now."

"John. I hope you're not thinking what I think you're thinking." Mantle said suddenly his voice filled with alarm.

"Oh but I am." Hunt said, a slow, sly smile spreading across his face. "I think it's time I faced my demons."

Chapter 23

Mantle was not a happy man. He had spent the past hour making his displeasure known, all to no avail. Despite the apparently reckless nature of Hunts' proposal there was no reasonable alternative that the ageing MI5 agent could produce. With the day marching inexorably on, he had to finally concede defeat. In order for Hunts' plan to work, there was a lot they had to accomplish that day.

Cunningham followed after Mantle as they left the clowns' caravan. He wasn't sure why exactly, but it seemed they were about to commandeer the circus and Mantle felt that a

Detectives' badge would prove useful in this regard.

"Can you explain this to me again please?" He asked Mantle as they crossed the grass, heading towards the managers trailer.

"All you need to know for the moment Detective is that we need to close the show today. No performances, no visitors, no nothing. We cannot afford to have any bystanders around when things start tonight."

"That's the part I'm still not clear on." Cunningham confessed. "What is supposed to happen tonight?"

"Truth be told young man, I'm not entirely sure myself."

"Surely you've done this before?"

"Whatever gives you that idea?" Mantle smirked.

"And Hunt?" Mantles blank look was all the answer Cunningham needed. "So why the hell are we trusting him with this then?"

"Because he is the only person who has the power to do what needs to be done."

"And if he gets it wrong?"

Mantle stopped at the door to the managers' trailer. He turned to Cunningham before knocking, his face deadly serious.

"That would be a very bad thing." He said softly.

The show manager was not at all happy with the appearance of the two men, and even less so when she realized their intent. There was, however, very little she could do in the face of both the law and the government. Even so, it still took no small amount of charm from Mantle and the promise of compensation to win her over.

Hunt watched the days' proceedings from the comfort of the clowns' caravan. The show was officially closed for the day. Various members of the team were assigned the task of turning away visitors and refunding advance tickets for disappointed customers, while other members of the circus team, under Mantles' direction, set about preparing the tent for the evenings' events.

Neither Hunt nor Mantle really had any idea what would happen that night, but they both agreed that it would be best if the mirror were placed out in the open. The clowns caravan was simply too confining. The tent seemed an ideal alternative. It was sheltered and provided concealment from prying eyes while, at the same time, allowing ample space for whatever may occur.

As the day wore on, Hunt found himself with very little to do except watch, wait and ponder. He had heard and subsequently overrode all of Mantles' objections, yet this did not mean he was without doubts of his own. The plan was reckless and dangerous, he would be the first to admit, yet, for reasons he could not clearly express, Hunt was certain it would work. The fact that Mantle was not in agreement did not unduly worry him, knowing, as he did, that Mantle did not have all the facts.

There was one key element that Hunt had neglected to share with his former doctor. It was something that had been playing through his mind throughout the day. The strange dream, if indeed dream it was, that he had experienced the previous evening. The image of the young, white robed girl had stayed with him. It was strangely comforting and something he really didn't feel inclined to share with anyone.

As important as the girls' memory was to him however, it was superseded by her words. That last message which had hung, just on the edge of hearing as she faded away into nothingness.

"If you fall, I will catch you."

Those words had drifted back into his consciousness that morning as the group was discussing what to do about the mirror. From that moment he had known exactly what was required of him.

Cunningham watched the two clowns carry the large oval mirror into the circus tent from his position midway up the center seating bank. Mantle had spent some time with the shows electrician arranging the lighting within the tent so that the large spotlights came together in the center of the ring, creating a single point of brilliant, white light approximately two meters in diameter. It was in the center of this pool of light that the clowns, exhibiting great care, laid the mirror, face upwards. The light level within the tent increased noticeably, the mirrored glass reflecting the focused beams to dramatic effect.

Apparently satisfied, Mantle left the lighting booth situated atop the central seating bank and joined the Detective further down.

"I think we're ready." He said with some satisfaction.

"Really?" Cunningham asked. Mantle noted the man's tone.

"You sound disappointed." He said reprovingly.

"I guess I am." The Detective admitted.

"What were you expecting?"

"I don't know. Candles, incense, maybe even a pentagram or two." Mantle laughed.

"You've been watching too many movies I'm afraid."

"Oh," Cunningham responded, looking a little crestfallen.

"Opiate for the masses, dear boy." Mantle explained, smiling broadly. "All of that ritual and paraphernalia is utter nonsense really."

"So what happens now then?"

"Now we wait." Mantle said seriously.

"For what exactly?"

"This is Hunts' show now. I think we're both going to have to wait and see how it all plays out." The old man mused. "Whatever happens though, I want you to stay close to me, understood?"

"Not really, no" Cunningham admitted. "But that's been a common theme today."

The sun had long since dropped over the horizon by the time Hunt fell asleep. It had been with some degree of trepidation that he had lain down on the big double bed in the clowns' master bedroom, fully expecting that blissful state to elude him entirely. Apparently he was far more fatigued than he had realized as he found himself enfolded in sleeps' gentle embrace almost the instant his head hit the pillow.

He could not have slept for long however, it still being pitch black within the caravan when he opened his eyes. Rising from the bed was difficult, every movement an act of extreme effort. He moved unsteadily through the caravan, heading for the exit.

Hunt was fighting to retain control of his thoughts. They were jumbled, erratic and incoherent. Flashing images from his past paraded endlessly before him. It felt as though someone were trolling through an image diary of his entire life, pausing briefly on selected images

depicting the worst moments. It was an endless gallery of grief. Deep down, Hunt knew what was happening. The Cloyne had broken into his sleep and was
using these images to manipulate his mood. The waves of despair and grief they generated were almost crippling. All Hunt wanted to do was to stop the show.

Cunningham and Mantle stood, hidden in the darkened entrance to the circus tent, the two clowns standing just behind them. The remaining circus members had been banished to their caravans earlier that evening, ostensibly for their own safety, although Cunningham suspected that Mantle didn't want any more witnesses to the evenings' events than were absolutely necessary.

The four men observed Hunts progress in silence as he exited the caravan, heading towards the Detectives' Ford Focus which had been parked on the grass nearby earlier that day.

"Here we go." Mantle breathed softly.

Once behind the wheel, Hunt started the engine and, with a ground-churning spin of the wheels, sped off into the night.

The maelstrom of images spun through Hunts' mind with abandon, building a wave of despair and grief that threatened to overwhelm him. He was driven onwards by that wave, driven towards the only escape, the only solution. New images began to appear, seemingly random pictures thrown in amongst the madness that was his existence. Cliff-tops, shorelines, high, raging seas. They were a message, telling Hunt where he must go. Leading him to the one place where he could bring the madness to an end, the one place where he could find peace.

For the second time in two days Hunt found himself at Beachy Head. The Ford was parked in an almost identical fashion to Caroline's Volvo the previous evening. Door open, lights on, simply abandoned in the mans' haste to be free of his despair.

There was no pause, no hesitation and no last minute reprieve. Hunt simply walked, resolutely, straight off the cliff. Without even being aware of it, Hunt had taken the small wooden disc out of his pocket as he had approached the cliff. At the very last minute, as he had stepped off into space, Hunt had released the disc, letting it tumble to the ground in a manner that closely mirrored his own graceless descent.

For a time, nothing moved. The cliffs remained bathed in darkness with only the gentle swish of the waves below intruding upon the silence. The small wooden disc had come to rest in the grass atop the cliffs edge while Hunts' broken and bloodied body lay, cruelly twisted on the rocks below.

Only those gifted with Hunts' unique vision could have borne witness to what happened next. A dark cloud seemed to flow out of Hunts body, dull, and pulsating with a deep red color. The sheer force of negative emotion had taken on a quasi-physical form, a form composed of all the despair, anguish and pain Hunt had ever felt.

It rose swiftly, ignorant of prevailing air currents, drawn onwards and upwards as if pulled by a magnet, finally coming to a stop only a few feet above the cliff edge. There was a slight pause as the cloud hovered above the wooden disc. Just at that moment a small, silvery ball of light shot out from Hunts body. Moving at incredible speed upwards, tracing the same path as the red cloud. Without any sign of resistance, the silver light entered the red cloud, allowing itself to become engulfed within its dark folds, coming to a stop at its heart. It was then

that the cloud descended, forming that same elongated funnel that Hunt had witnessed the previous evening. In a matter of only a few seconds, both the cloud and the silver light had been absorbed into the disc which then began to gradually fade, the air around it seeming to shimmer slightly. Then it was gone.

Back in the circus tent Cunningham and Mantle were seated on the front row of the left side seating bank, the father and son clown team seated opposite them on the colorful wooden boxes that formed the circus ring. Mantle was nervous. The Detective could feel the tension emanating from the old man. It was a tension, a nervousness he did not share. For his part, Cunningham was bored.

He didn't know how long they had waited since Hunts' departure but, for him, it was long enough. He began to rise, intending to stretch his legs when he saw it. There was no flash of light, no cloud of brimstone, in fact nothing to mark any change at all. In many ways, it was actually very disappointing.

"Mantle." He said softly nevertheless.

"I see it." The old man responded.

"What does it mean?" Cunningham asked.

"It means that he succeeded." Mantle answered sadly. "Mr. Hunt is dead."

They both sat in silence staring at the oval mirror which lay peacefully, bathed in light. Where once there had been a flaw, a perfectly circular hole in the frame, now, there was nothing, not even the merest crack to indicate that imperfection had ever existed.

Chapter 24

There was nothing. No sound. No light. No warmth. No cold. No sensation of any kind. All that remained was awareness, thought and feeling. It took a few moments before Hunt recalled what had happened. He had died, again.

The bone-shattering impact on the rocks below the cliffs played out briefly in his consciousness, but there was no pain. There was a vague recollection then, of being pulled, drawn away from himself, then a sudden moment of clarity. The girl.

"Shh John."

There was no voice to be heard, more like the memory of a voice implanted into his thoughts.

"You followed me?" Hunt sent out the silent question.

"You knew I would."

"Yes. I did." Hunt agreed.

"Do you know where you are, John?" She asked then. Hunt allowed his consciousness to range out, testing the boundaries of this new and strange environment.

"I think so." He said eventually. "We're inside the mirror, aren't we?"

"That's right." She confirmed. "We have entered the creatures' prison."

"It seems endless."

"It is not."

Hunt did not feel he was in a position to argue with the girl. She seemed to be aware of so much more than he was at the moment.

"Where is the creature then, this Cloyne?"

"It has sensed your presence John. Even now it draws near."

"Good." Hunt said firmly. "It's time to end this."

"That will not happen here. In this reality, you do not have that power."

"So what am I doing here then?" Hunt asked.

"You must find the borders of this prison. When you do, you will understand. But you must hurry. In this environment you are vulnerable to the creatures' power, and, if you die here, you will not return."

"And what will you do while I am looking for this "border"?"

"What I was created to do. I will protect you, for as long as I can. But hurry now, John. The creature is almost upon us."

The urgency in her voice was something that Hunt felt rather than heard. He understood the reason. There had been a steadily growing presence, cruel, malevolent and oppressive. As he allowed his awareness to reach out into the void, Hunt began to wonder if he had made a mistake.

It had made perfect sense at the time. They couldn't bring the creature back into the real world. That was far too dangerous. Someone had to face it on its own ground. Ultimately, he was the only person with the power, the ability to do that. It was only now that he was here, contained within the same void as the creature itself, that Hunt understood the reasons for Mantles' reservations. This was so far beyond anything he had experienced, anything he could have imagined even. If he could not destroy the demon here, however, then what else could he do? He pushed his awareness out further and further, searching desperately.

"What am I looking for?" He asked.

"Understand the nature of this place John, then you will know what you seek."

"I HUNGER!!"

There was an almost physical weight to the oppressive nature of this new presence. The creature was upon them. Hunt was aware of its not so subtle probing at the edges of his consciousness.

"Food, yes!!" The demon hissed, its desire almost palpable. "I must feed."

The creatures' presence closed in around him. It was a feeling of suffocation. There was no other way of describing what was happening. His entire consciousness was being smothered. There was an almost physical sensation of tearing as a piece of himself was broken away from the whole, a morsel to sate the creatures' appetite. The sensation was an obscene one and Hunt pitied those who had come before him. This was worse than any death he could envision. Having ones personality, one's essence, ones very soul being consumed piecemeal in this manner was a sensation beyond imagining.

"WHAT IS THIS?" The creature bellowed in surprise, withdrawing suddenly. Hunt felt the smothering weight of its presence lift. "I cannot feed on this."

"No demon, you cannot." The girls' voice was strong and calm. Hunt instinctively used this moment of respite to continue exploring his unusual surroundings.

"But I sense food. Why can I not feed? "There was a note of almost child-like petulance to the question.

"Your food is here, and it is rich. Despair, grief and death, all those morsels you desire so much. They are all here. Can you sense them Demon?"

"Yes." The creature said, longingly. "So sweet they are. I sense them. I need them. I want them."

"But you cannot have them."

"WHY?" The demon screamed in frustration.

The girl was taunting the creature, Hunt realized. She intended to keep its' thoughts off balance and unfocussed in the hopes that this would make his task easier. It was a dangerous game and they both knew it. Hunt continued his exploration with renewed urgency.

"You know why." The girl said simply. "There is something else here."

"Yes."

"Something that blocks your path."

"Yes."

"Something that denies you."

"YES."

"Can you feel it demon?"

"YES."

"Do you know what it is?"

There was a pause. Hunt felt the demon reaching out once more with its awareness. It was more cautious this time, gently easing forwards. But to no avail. The instant it came into contact with them it recoiled with a cry of pain and bewilderment.

"POISON" It cried. "WHY?" The cry was so mournful that, at that moment Hunt almost felt pity for the creature. "Centuries I have been held against my will, pitiful morsels my only sustenance. And now, now I am sent this!"

There was something new impinging just on the edge of Hunts' awareness now. It could only be described as a void within the void, an area of space where the creature could not, or would not enter. Something lay beyond this empty space. Hunt reached out further.

"I sense the ripest of fruits before me." The creature continued. "Yet I cannot taste of their bounty. Why torture me so? What purpose does it serve?"

"This from one who has tortured so many in the past?" The girl asked.

"I do not torture. I feed. It is my nature."

"You feed on the hate, the grief and the despair of others."

"Yes." The creature responded, its voice filled with a wistful longing. "Such fine sweetmeats. But none so fine as those I now sense. I must have them. Let me have them."

"They are protected." The girl insisted resolutely.

"NO!" The creature raged, reaching out for a third time.

"They are protected." The girl persisted. "By love, by joy and, most of all, by hope. They are protected."

"IT BURNS!" The creature screamed, recoiling once more.

Hunt finally understood what he was looking for. He had seen it before when he first examined the mirror. The faint silvery lattice around its frame. He could sense it now, just on the far side of the empty void. This was what the creature feared. As he probed further, Hunt began to understand the true nature of the barrier that formed the beasts' prison.

This was more than mere energy. There was a presence there as well. This was the entire life force of the mirrors' creator. He had used his own essence, his life force to form this prison, pouring all of his energy into the barrier that now lay just at the edge of Hunts' awareness. As Hunt continued to probe the barrier he felt the remnants of its creator, glimpsed briefly the fragments of memory that still remained. For two hundred years the craftsman had maintained this prison, sacrificing himself to contain the creature within its boundaries, protecting the world through this selfless act.

For a brief moment, as his awareness connected with that of the craftsman, Hunt reached a point of clarity. Two hundred years of accumulated wisdom passed to Hunt in that moment. All of the knowledge and experience the craftsman had gained in his own lifetime was now Hunts' to do with as he pleased. In that moment, Hunt understood exactly what was required of him. He had no power over the creature in this realm and no possibility of restoring the integrity of its prison. This left only one other option.

"Would you end your torment?" Hunt asked suddenly. The demon paused in its ravings, clearly unused to being spoken to in this manner.

"Well?" Hunt pressed.

"You seek to destroy me. I sense it." Hunt offered no response. "But you cannot harm me here. But I could consume you."

"You are correct." Hunt observed coolly. "On all counts. I cannot harm you in this place and, despite my protection you could and would eventually consume me. All of this is true. But what would you gain by that? You would remain here, trapped, perhaps forever. Is that what you want?"

"I need to feed." The creature answered simply.

"I know.".

The girl had remained silent throughout this exchange.

"You understand now, don't you John?" She asked.

"I think so." Hunt confirmed.

"Can you do what needs to be done?"

"I'm not sure." Hunt admitted. "But I don't think I have any other choice."

Until now Hunt had only ever drawn energy from his surroundings as an instinctual act, and then only in response to severe injury. He had never consciously attempted to control this power, until now.

The knowledge and experience he had gained from the craftsman's essence had shown him that he was capable of so much more. His ability could be controlled and manipulated in ways he had never even considered before. But he had to consider it now. Gathering his will, Hunt intertwined his own essence with that which formed the barrier. Then, with no warning, he began to absorb the essence into himself.

255 | Fool In The Ring

Chapter 25

The explosion ripped through the circus tent like a thunderclap, despite the fact that its actual concussive force was minimal, limited to an area of only a few feet from the oval mirror.

"Bloody hell!" Cunningham exclaimed, jumping to his feet.

The two clowns, sitting at the edge of the ring, both dived for cover, peeking their heads fearfully over the low, wooden border.

"What just happened?" Cunningham asked as he bounded towards the ringside with Mantle following just behind.

"I'm not entirely sure." The old man admitted.

In the center of the ring the dust began to settle. The mirror had been reduced to kindling and tiny shards of glass that sparkled, diamond-like in the intense light. All of this escaped the attention of the four observers however. Their eyes were drawn collectively to the dark cloud that rose above the scene of destruction. It swirled and undulated in a disturbing fashion and, at its center there pulsed a beating heart of deepest red.

Before anyone could react to this new phenomenon, a tendril reached out from the cloud. Moving lightning fast and with unerring accuracy it snared the old clown around the waist, hoisting him high into the air above the ring.

"Father!" The younger clown rose to his feet, preparing to launch himself into the ring. Mantle took a firm grasp on his arm.

"NO, boy!" He snapped harshly. "There's nothing you can do now.

"What the hell is that thing?" Cunningham asked in a voice that quavered with fear and awe.

Mantle did not answer, he simply watched with horrified fascination as the cloud rose to meet its captive.

"My God, John." He whispered finally. "What have you done?"

Cunningham moved to assist Mantles' efforts in restraining the young clown, all the while their eyes never leaving the malevolent cloud above them.

"Tell me this is supposed to be happening." Cunningham almost whispered.

"I wish I could." Mantle confessed curtly.

Without warning the clouds core suddenly pulsed brightly and, in a single movement, it engulfed the old clown completely.

"NO!" The son screamed in anguish.

Mantle became aware of movement to his left. Casting his eyes quickly in that direction he noted, with some surprise, the appearance of some of the circus troupe.

"Cunningham." He breathed. The Detective followed his gaze.

"What the hell?" He moved to intercept them, but Mantle stopped him.

"Wait." The old man said urgently. "Take a good look at them."

Cunningham frowned slightly. He hadn't noticed it at first but, to a man, the troupe moved in complete unison. Their gait was unnaturally stiff and, upon closer inspection he saw the same expressionless mask upon each of them.

"Are they asleep?" He asked. Mantle nodded.

"Maybe, or at least something like sleep." He mused thoughtfully. "Did you notice the glow?"

He was right, Cunningham saw on closer inspection. It was incredibly faint which was why the Detective hadn't spotted it at first. Each of them was surrounded by a delicate, silvery aura that seemed to sparkle whenever the light struck them.

"What's that all about?" He asked.

"I have absolutely no idea." Mantle confessed.

Sean, the younger clown, had, by now, collapsed to his knees, unable to look at his father any more. He cradled his head in his hands and wept openly. Meanwhile, above them, the cloud was slowly dissipating. As the last, greying wisps disappeared the figure that remained dropped heavily to the ground in the center of the ring, drawing all eyes towards it.

What had fallen from the cloud, and now rose steadily from the ground, no longer bore any resemblance to the old clown. At its full height, almost eight feet tall, it dominated the ring. Humanoid in form, it was garbed in a grotesque parody of an ancient clown costume, all ruffs and billowing, shiny, varicolored fabrics. The face was painted in a traditional white, with dark liner around the eyes and mouth and a single, black, five-pointed star covering the left eye. The creature was brutish, with a bulging, uneven musculature that seemed to writhe beneath its clothing in a disturbingly irregular fashion. As it turned to face the three men, they could see the incredible hunger in its large, blood red eyes.

"Is that…..?" Cunningham whispered fearfully

"The Cloyne." Mantle confirmed curtly. "John set it loose and I guess it needed someone to give it physical form. A host."

"The old man?"

"He already had a connection to the Cloyne." Mantle answered.

"So where is he now?"

"In there." Mantle indicated the huge creature dominating the center of the ring. "Somewhere."

"FREE" the creature boomed. It's voice low and gravelly. "And I hunger." Bowing its head it moved towards the three men.

The Cloyne had barely even completed its first step when three orbs of silvery light, no bigger than tennis balls, fired past it. They found their marks swiftly, striking each of the three men squarely in the chest. From that point the silvery light spread outwards rapidly encasing the men from head to toe.

"I can't move." Cunningham realized quickly. His voice showed him to be on the verge of panic.

"I know." Mantle said softly. "Neither can I. Keep calm. This is not the creatures doing."

"How do you know?"

"Because if it was, we would already be dead."

Cunningham had to concede the logic of this statement. He made a concerted effort to take control of the rising fear.

The creature, meanwhile, had halted its advance, confused by the unexpected light show.

"Who dares…" It began, its voice low and dangerous.

"I do." This voice was cold, strong, full of resolve and it belonged to Hunt "We have unfinished business, you and I." The Cloyne turned, enraged.

At first, there was nothing to be seen and this confused the Cloyne. Both Mantle and Cunningham tried to locate the source of their companions' voice, to no avail.

The light beams around the center of the ring continued to sparkle with what Mantle had assumed were the remnants of the shattered mirror, minute glass fragments refracting the light in a myriad of ways. Then the fragments moved. Almost as one, they began to draw together, gradually forming into a clearly defined shape, that shape becoming an image, that image becoming a man, a man they all recognized.

"Hunt." Cunningham breathed in amazement. Mantle merely smiled with satisfaction and no small amount of relief.

The Hunt that now stood before the beast, however, was not the one they remembered. He was, quite literally, a shadow of his former self.

It was like viewing a black and white hologram, real in every way, except for substance.

"You would seek to stop me?" The Cloyne asked incredulously.

"I must." Hunt replied simply.

"But you are nothing more than a shade, a memory. You cannot harm me."

"That may be true." Hunt conceded. "But as long as I exist, you will not be allowed to harm those under my protection."

"I will not be denied!" The creature raged.

It turned away from Hunt, raising its left arm towards the three men. A bolt of red-black energy fired out from the creatures' palm, aimed directly at Cunningham. The Detective squealed as the bolt struck him in the chest. He fully expected to be immolated on the spot, yet there was nothing. No sensation of impact, no indication of injury or pain, simply nothing. The silvery glow seemed to completely absorb the bolt on impact.

"Fascinating." Mantle breathed.

The Cloyne turned silently back to face his tormentor, his expression one of grudging respect.

"I know not how you have accomplished this." The creature said. "But I will allow you your victory. I would leave this place now, and feast elsewhere."

"I'm sorry." Hunt responded with genuine regret. "But that I cannot allow."

Unnoticed by all, the circus troupe had continued to file into the tent. Everyone was there, even the show manager herself, all asleep and totally unaware. They had positioned themselves evenly around the ring, forming a silvery circle that now was complete.

As Hunt looked at them, his altered vision revealed something that was hidden from the other observers. Where all saw a silvery, glowing light surrounding each person, Hunt saw a collection of young girls, the same girls whose souls had been freed from the candle. They were each offering the last of their life force to protect their charges. They each did this willingly as was evidenced by the peaceful, benevolent smiles they wore.

"What trickery is this?" The Cloyne demanded.

The circus troupe, on some hidden signal, reached out to one another, joining hands, making the circle complete. The Cloyne watched with mounting confusion as beams of light seemed to curve upwards and inwards from each of the figures, connecting eventually at a point twenty feet above their heads. Then, from the apex downwards, crisscrossing beams of light formed between the main light spars. They formed an interwoven lattice that reached ultimately to the ground. The entire effect was one of a silvery, lattice dome, a barrier under which stood The Cloyne and Hunt.

It was only at the last moment that the Cloyne understood what had happened. His eyes burned with intense hatred as he turned to face an unconcerned looking Hunt.

"Why?" The creature rasped, moving towards the shadowy Hunt. "Why free me from one prison, only to place me inside another?"

"It was necessary." Hunt answered with no hint of fear in either voice or demeanor.

"NO!!" The creature bellowed, firing another dark beam from its palm. This it aimed at Hunt. A look of momentary
surprise crossed the mans' face as the beam passed directly through his chest, connecting

eventually with the silvery barrier at the edge of the ring where it was absorbed harmlessly.

"I must feed." The creature pleaded desperately. Hunt said nothing.

Hunt watched as the creature began to pace erratically around the ring.

"It frees me then it traps me again." The Cloyne ranted, gesticulating wildly. The creature was clearly mad, that much Hunt already knew, but, as he watched it now, he realized something else. Although ancient, the beasts' intellect and emotional level was little more than that of a child. And, like any other child, it reacted poorly when denied. What Hunt witnessed now was the beasts' equivalent of a temper tantrum. In other circumstances it might have been amusing, but not here, and not now.

"It knows I must feed, yet it stops me. They always stop me. But this one is nothing. It is a shade, it has no power. It cannot hurt me."

Hunt was the first to notice movement at the main entrance to the circus tent. What he saw there surprised even him.

It was a small, silent, silvery procession. The girl from his dream on the balcony led the way.

Behind came six of her companions arranged two abreast, bearing above their heads a sight that Hunt hoped fervently he would never have to see again.

It was difficult to describe the emotions Hunt felt as he
watched his own body being borne by this somber procession. They glided smoothly towards the ring. It was only as they reached the barrier that the creature became aware of their presence. Its brow furrowed with obvious confusion as the group passed, unhindered through the barrier.

"What new mischief is this?" It demanded.

Hunt could not answer. The sight of his own bloodied and broken form drawing ever closer had him completely entranced. He watched with a macabre fascination as his body was laid at his own shadowy feet.

"John." The girl whispered softly, tearing Hunts' gaze away from the vision his mind was struggling to comprehend. She smiled as he brought his eyes up to meet hers, drawing strength from that brief connection. "It is time to end this."

Hunt nodded in understanding. He closed his eyes, concentrating all of his thought and energy on the task at hand.

The sudden pain threatened to completely overwhelm him. Every nerve in his body screamed its displeasure. His six ghostly pall bearers moved instantly, surrounding his body with their silvery, ethereal glow. Almost immediately the pain began to recede, enough at least that Hunt could think coherently once more.

Hunt needed to heal, his body cried out for the necessary energy. In the past he had always acted on pure instinct, reaching out to forcefully take what his battered form craved and, in so doing, he had destroyed those from whom he had fed. Tonight was different. Hunt still retained the knowledge and experiences gained from absorbing the craftsman's essence.

He now knew how to control his power and, with the soothing presence of the young girls enabling him to override his natural impulses, he had the time to exercise that control.

As Hunt lay on his back, his broken body immobilized, the six young girls knelt down next to him, three on each side. One by one, they each laid a delicate, ghostly hand upon his chest. He looked at their smiling faces, their gentle eyes displaying nothing but warmth and affection for the man that had been their savior. They nodded in unison, bowing their heads in acceptance of what was to come and Hunt, with a grateful tear rolling down his cheek, understood. He allowed his essence to reach out to them.

Until now Hunt would have described the act of forcefully drawing out a persons' essence as not unlike drawing a nail out of ones' own flesh. There was that moment of excruciating pain as the offending object was withdrawn followed by a sense of overwhelming relief as the healing process could begin. The feelings he experienced now were very different indeed.

All that remained of the six young girls they offered freely and willingly up to him. There was no resistance, only a grateful, almost loving acceptance. Their energy suffused his being, filling him with a warmth and grace he had never before known. All the while his body began the process of repair. Limbs, once separated, became joined, shattered bones knitted themselves back together, muscle, skin and sinew regrew.

The Cloyne watched all of this with an almost child-like wonderment, unable to fully comprehend what it witnessed. It was only as Hunt, born anew, began to rise, that the creature realized the potential threat he now posed.

Acting purely on instinct, the Cloyne lashed out, a great bolt of dark energy blasting out from his palms. The bolt never found its mark, striking instead the glowing form of the young girl. She blocked its path, absorbing the energy easily. The creature growled its face full of anger and resentment.

"The shade becomes a man." It hissed. "But not a true man I think. You and I are the same. We are both parasites to this world. We feed on the weak, the helpless. What gives you the right to interfere with me now?"

"Are we the same?" Hunt asked, now fully healed. "Perhaps." He began moving towards the center of the ring, the Cloyne turning to follow his every move. By the time he reached the circle of brilliant light he had left the protection of the young girl. Now Hunt stood alone, bloodied still, his clothes torn, but whole once more.

"There is one important difference however." Hunt noted coldly. "My hunger has been sated. Can you say the same?"

He was deliberately goading the Cloyne now, and the creature, with its infantile intellect, responded exactly as he had hoped.

"I must FEED!" The creature stormed, almost incoherent with rage.

"Then feed now Cloyne! What's stopping you? Take what you need from me! I have no protection. I cannot oppose you! Or, are you afraid of me?"

The Cloyne required no further urging. Acting on the same kind of instinctive level that Hunt knew only too well, the creature launched a single tendril of dark energy from its hand. The tendril thrust itself into Hunts' chest causing him to cry out in pain, but he stood his ground.

Hunt was now on the wrong side of a feast. He realized with horror what it must have felt like for his own victims. The tendril connecting them both throbbed and pulsed as it began to drain the darkest of energies from Hunt.

The creatures' eyes widened in ecstasy as it got its first taste of the darkness that was its victim. Hunt felt himself fading with each passing second. He dropped to his knees, casting a concerned look towards the young girl who had remained to the side of the ring, watching impassively. She nodded her face unreadable.

With a deep breath Hunt reached up and grasped the tendril with both hands.

"Are you enjoying your feast?" He shouted, his breaths coming in short gasps now as the energy left him.

"So sweet." The creature exalted, its eyes closed, savoring every moment.

"I'm glad you like it." Hunt growled, taking deep breaths and gathering what little energy now remained within him. "But I want it back now!" So saying, Hunt focused every ounce of his being upon that umbilical-like tendril, concentrated everything he was upon the dark energy flowing through it.

The pulsing of the tendril gradually slowed then stopped entirely. The Cloynes eyes snapped open, ablaze with fury.

"I WILL HAVE MY FOOD!" The creature bellowed.

"NO!" Hunt countered. "This is my pain, my despair, my sorrow, and I will have it back!"

The struggle began in earnest then, as both fought for control. They were surprisingly evenly matched. Hunt was weak, having already conceded a large portion of his energy to the creature. The Cloyne however, had spent over two hundred years in a magical prison, feeding only on isolated morsels. Even with the addition of Hunts' energy, it was visibly struggling.

Hunt had one further advantage however, and it was this that proved to be the deciding factor. The creature had been right. They were the same in many respects. They both fed on energy and, until today at least, they were both creatures of instinct. Where they differed was that Hunt had the capacity to learn and, through learning, to evolve. During the course of this encounter Hunt had learnt control. He could consciously manipulate and use his ability now in ways the creature could never match, or even understand.

Gritting his teeth in determination Hunt focused his entire being on the energy that filled the umbilical that connected him to the beast. The tendril began to pulse, slowly at first, seconds passing between each beat. Gradually the pulsing increased in frequency, as it did so, the energy began to flow once more, only now the direction of flow had reversed.

"NO!" The creature cried plaintively as it felt the strength leaving it.

Hunt mercilessly maintained his resolve. With each passing second he grew stronger and the flow increased in speed, the tendrils' pulses coming with ever greater frequency. But there was still more.

Hunt had allowed the creature to attack him for a reason.

He had wanted the Cloyne to open a conduit between them, had wanted it to feed upon him. It was the only way he could have gained access to the creatures own energy. As the creature, lost in its' feeding ecstasy, drew more and more of Hunt to itself, Hunt had manipulated his own energy. In much the same way as a fisherman would bait a worm on a hook Hunt had woven his energy around that of the Cloyne, interweaving them to the point where it was almost impossible to determine where one began and the other ended. Now, as Hunt withdrew his line, that metaphorical hook was performing exactly as he had hoped. As Hunts own energy returned, it drew the Cloyne with it.

Hunt now found himself battling on two fronts. He fought, on the one hand, to draw the creature from its current host while, on the other, he struggled to maintain control of himself as the creature, realizing Hunts' intent, was now using what power remained to attack Hunt directly.

The Cloyne's host had been steadily reducing in size as more and more of the creature was drawn out of it. Its form changed constantly now, reverting gradually back to its original state. As the last vestiges of the Cloyne were ripped away, all that remained was the old clown who dropped, lifeless to the ground.

Within Hunt the battle raged on. Both the Cloyne and Hunt fought desperately for survival and Hunt knew that, if left unaided, he would certainly loose this fight. He had no intention, however, of allowing that to happen. As soon as he felt the last of the Cloyne enter his being, he threw his arms wide, raised his head to the heavens and cried out a single word.

"NOW!"

Instantly, the silvery cage that had surrounded them this entire time, began to collapse. The silvery lattice disappeared completely while, at the same time the apex point, formed by those individual shafts of light, descended rapidly, bringing each of those beams with it.

Hunt watched it descend, closing his eyes as the light touched onto his forehead, focusing all those beans to that single point. All of the young girls that had stood protecting their individual charges at the ringside, now focused all of their remaining energy entirely upon Hunt. The light intensified, becoming so bright that the three living observers were forced to close their eyes. It grew and grew, bathing Hunts' entire form in its radiance.

This alone was not enough. Hunt knew that, as long as the Cloyne remained within a host, in this case him, it was protected. There was still one final task Hunt needed to perform if he were to finally destroy this creature.

With a final, supreme effort Hunt used all of his energy and will to force the creature from him. The creature's essence, forcefully ejected from this new host, formed into a pulsating cloud once more that hovered in the air above Hunt's head.

With no host to protect it, the creature was vulnerable. Before it could react the brilliant light encircled it completely.

The Cloyne saw the light building all around it, closing in from every direction. It was like pouring foam over a raging fire. There was nowhere for the Cloyne to retreat to, no possibility of escape. The intense brilliance smothered the creature in its entirety, leaving nothing in its wake.

Then the light was gone, blinking out in an instant. The battle was over, the creature vanquished. All that remained was Hunt, kneeling in silence in the center of the ring.

Chapter 26

For a brief moment, it felt to Hunt as though time had stopped. He fought to control his breathing before finally looking up and taking stock of his surroundings.

Mantle and Cunningham were both moving quickly around the ring, administering to the assembled troupe. With the disappearance of the silvery apparitions everyone had been freed from their trance-like state. There was a lot of confusion and shaking of heads as the two men gradually herded everyone out of the tent and back to their respective residences.

A low groan drew Hunts' attention back to the ring. Freed from the confining light, Sean had leapt the barrier, racing to his fathers' side. Hunt watched with an almost overwhelming sense of sadness and regret as the son rocked slowly back and forth on his knees, his fathers' head cradled in his lap. The moaning had been a vocal expression of the young clowns' grief as he gently stroked his fathers' face, tears streaming down his own.

"There was nothing you could do." The gentle voice came from Hunts' left side. He knew its' owner, the young girl. "He was not yours to save." She added with some sympathy.

"I know." Hunt said simply. "That doesn't really help though, does it?"

"I suppose not." The girl conceded.

"Was it worth it?"

"It was necessary."

"That's not really the same, and you know it." Hunt responded cynically.

"The Cloyne was a creature of another time, the last of his kind. It no longer had a place in this world."

"It was barely more than a child." Hunt objected. "It was an animal, doing only what it needed to survive. It was never evil. It couldn't even understand the concept."

"This has nothing to do with good and evil, John."

"If not that, then what?" Hunt asked.

"This world is constantly evolving, constantly changing. As it does so, occasionally things, beings get left behind. Most of the time they die out on their own, but sometimes they don't."

"So what am I, the worlds' executioner then?" Hunt asked bitterly.

"You are so much more than that, John." Hunt looked at her, the doubt evident on his face. "You will understand in time, but you must be patient. For the moment you should take comfort from the fact that no more lives will be destroyed by that creature. That is at least something don't you think?"

"I suppose so." Hunt conceded with a heavy sigh. "So what happens now?"

"You have a long and difficult road ahead of you John." The girl said gently. "Exactly where it will lead, I cannot say. There is one thing I do know however. Before your journey has reached its end, you will have need of my help again. When you do, rest assured, I will be there."

Hunt looked at her closely, a question forming on his lips. She smiled warmly.

"When I was alive, they called me Cheryl."

"Thank you, Cheryl." Hunt whispered to the empty air. In a heartbeat, she had gone.

By the time Mantle and Cunningham returned to the tent Hunt had picked himself up and moved across to take a seat in the stands. He watched impassively as Cunningham moved across to the young clown and his father.

"Well, that was certainly an eventful evening." Mantle said, taking a seat next to Hunt.

"That's one way you could put it." Hunt said evenly, his eyes never leaving the heartbreaking scene that played out in the ring. Mantle followed the younger mans' gaze.

"Every battle has its casualties." He said with a heavy sigh.

"That's easy to say when you're not the casualty in question, or the one mourning their loss."

"Perhaps." Mantle said softly, taking the rebuke in his stride.

They were both silent, watching as Cunningham quickly left the tent, returning only a few moments later with two paramedics in tow. It was a futile effort, Hunt knew.

"Tell me John." Mantle asked eventually. "How much of tonight did you actually plan?"

"Not as much as I would have liked." Hunt snorted.

"So you were "winging" it?"

"Pretty much." Hunt admitted.

"You know we're going to have to talk about what happened here tonight?" Mantle pressed.

"I know." Hunt acceded. "But not tonight, Doc. Not tonight." Hunt stood and began stepping down from the stands.

"Where are you going?" Mantle asked in sudden alarm.

"I need some air. I'll be back soon."

Mantle nodded in understanding. While he was concerned about his young companion, he understood the need Hunt had for some personal space. A lot had happened, probably far more than Mantle would ever know. It was going to take his former patient a little time to make sense of it all.

Leaving the circus ground behind Hunt was not really sure where he was going, content merely to walk, to enjoy the momentary night silence before the dawn broke and the daytime madness resumed. Having said that, he was not at all surprised when, upon looking up and taking stock of his surroundings, he found himself at Sovereign Harbor.

He smiled, a sense of peace filling him as he found a place along the rocky outcroppings where he could sit and watch the gentle roll of the waves. Unknowingly, his feet had brought him full circle, bringing the events of the last two days to a natural conclusion. While he was not entirely satisfied with the results, he had to admit to a deep sense of closure as he embraced the cooling salt spray that wafted gently across him.

"You've been busy."

Hunt almost laughed out loud when he heard the voice.

"I thought I'd be seeing you before too long." He said evenly without turning around.

"It seemed an appropriate time to pick up where we left off." The voice quipped good-naturedly.

Hunt turned finally. There he was, sitting calmly on a rock only a few feet away, and looking as grotesque as ever.

"You're not really Andrew, are you?" Hunt asked. For a moment the macabre creature looked surprised then he let out a horrible, wet, gurgling sound that Hunt took to be a laugh.

"Very good, John." He congratulated. "You have come a long way, I am impressed."

"So who are you, and why the charade?"

"I'll answer the second question first. This "charade" as you call it was necessary. When I first appeared to you I had two goals, I needed to shock you into action and I needed you to hear what I had to say. I felt those goals would have been easier to achieve if you were presented with a face you recognized. And, for the most part, I was right."

"Did you have to choose something so…. grotesque?"

"The choice of image was nothing to do with me. I took the strongest visual that you were projecting at the time. That's just the way it works."

Hunt remembered how he had been having a nightmare about the explosion just prior to "Andrews'" first visitation.

"Fair enough. What about the first question?"

"To be honest, as far as you've come, I still don't think you are quite ready to hear that yet."

"Of course not." Hunt noted sourly. "Heaven forbid I be given any kind of useful information."

"I'm not the one who really matters, John. You are." Hunt did not look very convinced. "Look, you've had your little strop, John. You've been allowed to run around for the past six weeks creating all kinds of mischief, and, hopefully, along the way, you've learnt a few things. So the simple question now is are you done? Are you ready to get back to work?"

"I might be able to answer that if I knew what this "work" was." Hunt stated petulantly, turning back to look out to sea.

"There is a war coming, John. Even now, sides are preparing troops and considering where to draw their battle lines."

"What, and I'm supposed to stop it?"

"No, John. That's not your task."

"Then what?"

Andrew paused, taking a moment to collect his thoughts before answering.

"Consider, John, a chess board."

"Pardon?" Hunt turned back, confusion written all over his face. Andrew held up a finger.

"Just work with me a moment, please." Hunt closed his mouth, swallowing his next comment. "A chess board. The game has just been played, one side has won, it doesn't matter which. What does matter is that at the end of the game there are still pieces in place on the board. Now, before a new game can start, before new pieces can be placed on the board, the old pieces, those that remained from the previous game, they have to be removed. That is where you come in."

Hunt thought about that statement for a few moments. Andrew could see the concentrated look on his face and he waited patiently for a response.

"Okay, so if I am to believe what you say, then there has been a similar war at some point in the past."

Andrew nodded wordlessly.

"And some of the "pieces" from that war are still here today?"

Another nod. Hunt looked up suddenly.

"The Cloyne?"

"Very good John." Andrew looked pleased.

"So I am expected to find the rest of these "pieces" and remove them?"

"That's correct."

"And just how am I supposed to find them?"

"I don't think you will have to worry about that, after all, you found the Cloyne and that was before you even knew about all this."

"That's true I suppose." Hunt conceded.

"There's something you need to be aware of John." Andrew cautioned. "Because of the nature of your role, you are not on anybody's side. Your task is to clear pieces from both sides and that puts you at odds with everyone."

"Oh that's just great." Hunt noted sourly. "So what, are you saying, I should be careful who I trust?"

"Oh no, John. I'm saying, don't trust anyone at all."

Hunt turned sharply at this statement, but Andrew was already gone.

"I hate it when you do that!" Hunt noted, bitterly addressing the empty air.

Chapter 27

A week had passed since the dramatic events in Eastbourne. There had been surprisingly little attention from the news outlets. Mantle had expended a great deal of energy in engineering an elaborate cover-up involving some kind of minor medical outbreak. Hunt had not really involved himself in the details.

Cunningham had proved to be a very useful asset during this time. Several days had been spent interviewing the members of the circus troupe, a task that the Detective was predictably well suited for. It was a matter of incredible good fortune that, with the exception of the young clown, all of them had no memory of the events that had taken place that night. Mantle suspected that the strange energy that had surrounded them all had a lot to do with their inexplicable and collective memory loss, although he wasn't going to complain about it.

Mantle had dealt with Sean. Hunt had no idea of the
content of their discussions but, by the end of it all, the young man had agreed that nothing would be gained by making a public spectacle out of everything. In truth, Hunt suspected that he was relieved it was all finally over. The clown family had lived under this shadow all of their lives. Now for the first time, there was perhaps the chance for a little bit of sunshine.

For Hunt, the past week had been blessedly uneventful. Almost as soon as he had returned from his stroll that night, Mantle had bundled him into his car and whisked him away. Now Hunt found himself sitting on a relatively comfortable wooden balcony chair, looking out across the river Thames. The two-bedroom apartment was extremely comfortable and, situated as it was in Canary Wharf, was well positioned for both privacy and quick access to transport options both nationally and internationally.

None of that really mattered to Hunt as he relaxed back with a glass of his beloved Bruichladdich. It was clear that Mantle was going to great pains to look after him. Shortly after arriving in London the old man had insisted on a new wardrobe for Hunt. Outfitters had arrived at the apartment later that same day and, Hunt had to admit, the results were more than satisfactory, although Mantle had not been overly impressed with some of Hunts style choices.

Currently he was dressed in a very relaxed fashion, stonewashed, blue denim jeans with a well pressed, white cotton shirt, open at the neck. A well-fitted tan, suede leather waistcoat and tan leather brogues completed his casual outfit.

Strangely, Hunt still wore gloves, although these were now close fitting, fine tanned leather. Sunglasses were also never far
from his reach, even now, sitting alone on the balcony, they lay just on the small wooden table to his left. Mantle had taken great pains to point out how unnecessary either accessory was and,

privately, Hunt agreed with his logic. His decision to retain these two items however, had nothing to do with logic.

Intellectually Hunt knew that his power was under his own control now and there was no inherent danger in physical contact. However, as much as the events on the circus had taught him how to control his new abilities, they had also taught him that he was now very different from the person he once was. He felt it, deep within the very core of his being. Each step he took on this strange and disturbing journey seemed to move him further and further away from humanity. The gloves in particular symbolized that separation. Hunt had never felt more alone. The sunglasses helped to reinforce that position. They discouraged people from getting too close to him and, after what had happened to Caroline that was more important than ever.

Despite the distance, Hunt heard the faint clicking of the latch on the apartment door. He turned slightly, glancing through the floor-to-ceiling glass windows, a look of mild irritation on his face at having this peaceful moment interrupted. Seeing that it was Mantle, Hunt turned back towards the sunset.

"You're looking very relaxed there, John." The former Doctor noted glibly. "Mind if I join you?"

"Be my guest. You're paying for it after all."

"That's very true." Mantle agreed, pouring himself a shot of Akvinta Vodka into a tumbler and bringing it over with him to the balcony.

"You're on your own." Hunt observed as Mantle relaxed into a chair with a heavy sigh.

"Yes. Cunningham will be joining us tomorrow." Hunt raised an eyebrow in surprise.

"I thought you'd have let him go by now."

"I'm finding the Detective to be rather useful actually."

"Really? So he's joining us then?"

"Yes, I've spent the past couple of days arranging the paperwork. As of tomorrow he will be officially under the purview of MI5. I just needed him to finish of a few things in Bath first."

"Jane?" Mantles' face fell at the mention of the name. "There's still no word then?" Hunt pressed.

"I'm afraid not" Mantle admitted.

"You're worried about her, aren't you?"

"To be perfectly frank, yes, I am. Don't misunderstand me. Jane is perfectly capable of taking care of herself. She is strong, skilled and very resourceful, but….."

"It's been too long." Hunt finished the sentence. Mantle nodded silently, not wanting to voice the possibilities for fear that the worst of them may prove to be true. Hunt felt a great well of sympathy for the old man.

"Don't worry Doc." He said softly, a hard edge to his voice. "We'll find her. I promise."

Chapter 28

As he relaxed back into the plush leather upholstery of the deep-seated armchair, Mr. Bera reflected on how much he really detested coming to this place. Full of opulence and grandeur, vaulted ceilings, expensive furnishings, it was a place designed to impress or intimidate, depending upon the guest. Mr. Bera felt neither emotion as he glanced scathingly around at the collection of Chippendale furniture. He knew it was all a sham, a Hollywood façade. This was the seat of power in what was still, laughingly termed, "Great Britain". Bera remembered a time when this tiny island really was Great and truly deserved the title. In more recent years however, this seat had proven to be far too large for its various occupants, the current one being no exception.

Bera looked up as the Prime Minister entered the room, his expression a carefully contrived blank mask designed to conceal his utter contempt. The most powerful man in the country indicated for his two guards to remain at the door,
this was to be a private conversation. Bera almost laughed at that thought. The illusion of power was never more apparent. The current Prime Minister was only one in a long line of men, chosen for certain qualities. He was little more than a lamb in wolves clothing, bought and paid for by individuals possessing of real power, and placed here to act as their mouthpiece.

"No-one saw you arrive?" The Prime Minister asked. Mr. Bera had to smile now. The man had elected to remain standing, looking down upon Bera in a manner which was intended to convey superiority. It wasn't working.

"The Cloyne has been defeated." Bera said in an offhand manner, deliberately ignoring the

Prime Ministers question. Bera was pleased at the look of shock that spread across the Prime Ministers' bland features.

"What? When did this happen?"

"Just over a week ago." Bera answered calmly.

"And, I'm only now hearing about it?"

"It changes nothing."

"How can you say that?" The Prime Minister was visibly taken aback, yet another sign of weakness.

"The Cloyne was never meant to be anything more than a distraction."

"This was Hunts' doing wasn't it?" Bera nodded. "He's moving too fast. We need to slow him down." There was an edge of panic to the mans' voice that made Bera wince. Looking at him now, it would have been difficult to believe that he was actually the leader of one of the most powerful nations in the Western world.

"Hunt is my problem, and I will deal with him."

"Make sure that you do." The Prime Minister snapped. "First Eve, now the Cloyne. You have continually underestimated this man and we cannot afford any more losses as a result of your failings."

"I don't need you to tell me what is at stake here." Bera said darkly. "I already have a plan in motion for Mr. Hunt."

"Well, work quickly. That man is coming into his power far quicker than we anticipated."

"That is very true. However, he still has no real idea of his purpose, and that gives me the advantage." Bera mused with a sly smile. "When do the Council next meet?"

"Two months from now."

"Good. By then I should have something positive to report." Bera stated confidently rising from his comfortable chair.

A short time later Mr. Bera was relaxing once more, this time in the back of his luxurious Limousine, a glass of sparkling mineral water in his hand. He idly thumbed the intercom switch connecting him to the driver.

"Have we had any word from Carl yet?" He asked.

"Yes sir." The driver responded quickly. "They left port thirty minutes ago."

"Excellent." Bera responded happily. "Head for Gatwick please. I have a plane to catch."

Epilogue

The "Côte Des Dunes" was already half way through her ninety minute voyage to Calais. Operating now under the French Flag, she had been in service since 2001. The ship was a fairly well-appointed car ferry with a range of amenities available for her passengers to pass the time during their brief journey across the channel.

Her captain was content with the ships progress so far. The seas were fairly calm and her four big engines propelled her easily across the water at a steady speed of twenty-three knots, falling just short of the ships maximum of twenty-five. There had been no problems at all on this crossing and the Captain did not expect any. For him it was entirely, business as usual.

The only unusual aspect of this journey was the presence of the ambulance on the car deck several stories below. While medical transportation in this manner was not unheard of, neither was it so commonplace as to be classified as routine. Still, all the paperwork was in order. A doctor and two
paramedics were travelling in the ambulance with the patient and all relevant identification had been checked. The port authorities were happy, which meant the Captain was happy.

The only person who was not entirely happy was the Doctor. He had entered the employ of Mr. Bera several years previously following a brief indiscretion with a young girl that had threatened his career. Mr. Bera had made the problem disappear and now the Doctor was bound to his service.

He sat in the back of the ambulance, a sullen expression on his face. He didn't feel that his presence was strictly necessary, but one didn't argue with Mr. Bera.

The young woman laid peacefully on the stretcher across from him had no obvious sign of injury. In fact, barring a small bruise on her jaw, she was in extremely good condition. The only instructions the Doctor had been given were that the woman was to remain sedated for the entirety of their journey. It was a simple enough task, one that could have been performed by any nurse. Still, the Doctor was being paid handsomely for his services, far more than he could have made in his own practice in a year. That made up for the inconvenience somewhat.

The Doctor looked across at the young woman, admiring her fine features, the long raven hair, her soft, alabaster skin. His eyes filled with longing. He cast a brief, irritated glance towards the front of the ambulance and the two "paramedics", neither man had spoken since they had boarded the ship. It was a shame they were here, the Doctor thought sourly. But for their presence, the trip might have had some definite possibilities.

"I don't know what you did to piss Mr. Bera off." The Doctor muttered softly, gazing lustfully at the young woman. "But I wouldn't want to be in your shoes right now."

Jane offered no response, but then, the Doctor would have been surprised if she had.

Currently she had enough sedative flowing through her veins to keep a bull elephant down for several hours. She simply lay in peaceful slumber, blissfully unaware of the events transpiring around her.

www.ingramcontent.com/pod-product-compliance
Lightning Source LLC
LaVergne TN
LVHW040041080526
838202LV00045B/3439